HOME IS THE OUTLAW

HOME IS THE OUTLAW

Lewis B. Patten

Chivers Press · G.K. Hall & Co.
Bath, Avon, England · Thorndike, Maine USA

This Large Print edition is published by Chivers Press, England, and by G.K. Hall & Co., USA.

Published in 1996 in the U.K. by arrangement with Catherine C. Patten.

Published in 1996 in the U.S. by arrangement with Golden West Literary Agent.

U.K. Hardcover ISBN 0–7451–3880–2 (Chivers Large Print)
U.S. Softcover   ISBN 0–7838–1520–4 (Nightingale Collection Edition)

The text of this Large Print edition is unabridged.
Other aspects of the book may vary from the original edition.

Set in 16 pt. New Times Roman.

Printed in Great Britain on acid-free paper.

British Library Cataloguing in Publication Data available

Library of Congress Cataloging-in-Publication Data

Patten, Lewis B.
    Home is the outlaw / by Lewis B. Patten.
        p.   cm.
    ISBN 0–7838–1520–4 (lg. print : lsc)
    1. Large type books.   I. Title.
[PS3566.A79H66   1996]
813′.54—dc20
                                                                    95–38041

CHAPTER ONE

Morgan Orr lost his pursuers at last, high on the snowy slopes of the Continental Divide where the air was windy and sharp with the coming of fall. He camped that evening as the sun set and built a small fire, the first in more than two weeks. Hunkered comfortably beside it, he stared through the thin, blue, rising spiral of smoke at the distant slopes below—slopes that were bright with the yellow of night-frosted aspen leaves, dark with the brooding color of pine and spruce.

He was a tall man just past thirty, and his brown, level eyes were sombre, his long, straight mouth a trifle bleak. Remembering, his mind stared along his twisting back-trail and he realized just how many times he had fled for his life—how many more he had stood spread-legged and fought for the same stake.

Morgan Orr was a man of the gun. You could see it in the watchfulness that never quite disappeared from his bony face however relaxed he might become. You could see it in the way his worn and weathered gun hung holstered at his side. You could feel it sometimes, too, just as you feel the feral wildness in a caged and pacing lion.

Yet now, with the dividing line of thirty behind him, there was something else apparent

1

in the man—brooding sadness, perhaps, at the vista which lay ahead—bitter knowledge that a man who lives by the gun must also, inevitably, die by it.

Other things were there—knowledge of what he was, what he had become in the ten long years since he left the dusty, sleepy streets of Arapaho Wells. Loneliness for friends he had never had, family closeness he had never known—a woman, a certain woman he had never been able to forget.

Thirty had a way of making a man see what had been missed along the way. Morgan Orr was seeing that and feeling an ache of emptiness that wouldn't go away.

Out there, on the far, tawny plains that were now blue and smoky with distance, Arapaho Wells still slumbered, probably unchanged by the passing years. It was a beacon in his mind—a symbol of stability and security.

He knew his concept of it was false. But as he hunkered there, he made up his mind that he'd go back. He'd go back now. If there was salvation for him anywhere, it was in Arapaho Wells.

At dark, he killed his fire, moved his wind-broken horse's picket stake—for grass was thin—and watched with pity and regret as the animal cropped it halfheartedly, then gave up and stood with his head hanging. Morgan had almost ridden him to death, without mercy, and he owed the horse his life.

He had no food, so he got his worn blanket from behind the saddle, wrapped himself in it and laid down on the rocky ground. All through the night he shivered there as cold seeped through the blanket, through his flesh, until it reached the very marrow of his bones.

He rose at dawn, giving a quick look at his horse to make certain the animal had made it through the night. Hungry, cold, irritable and depressed, he saddled up and began to walk, leading the horse, down the steep, bare slope toward the line of green at timberline.

Ten years. Ten long years of violence. Ten years while the name of Morgan Orr became known from one end of the frontier to the other. And it came to this, to a ragged, hungry man limping down the slope of the mountains toward a town that probably wouldn't even take him in.

But the thought of it was like a star before him, leading him on. He remembered Tena, and the mind-picture his thoughts conjured up put a sharp, painful ache in his chest.

Small, finely boned, dark of hair and eye. A full-lipped, generous girl, with small, high cheekbones and a strong, determined chin.

Tena, who had lain in his arms that night six years ago, more because she knew his need of her than because she needed him.

He understood that now; he hadn't then. And understanding, he felt a tenderness toward her never felt toward another human

3

being before.

Bare, high country gave way to scrubby brush and then to stunted pine. He crossed clear, tumbling streams, growing hungrier, and always alert for game. But it was as though he was fated to fail. He saw tracks and birds, but not another living thing.

Night, and he camped again, and went on in the morning, his horse growing ever weaker, his own belly cramping and jumping with hunger. His eyes grew overly bright, and he rode more often than he walked.

The mountains flattened to rounded hills. And at last he saw the plain, dropped onto it and rode ahead. Arapaho Wells was a picture before his eyes, its location as definite as though he had a map in his mind.

A rabbit jumped up before him and he drew and shot automatically with blinding speed. The rabbit fell in a crumpled heap.

Though it was only midmorning, Morgan dismounted, peeled the skin from the rabbit and built a small fire. He broiled the rabbit, but only partially, for his ravenous hunger wouldn't let him wait. Then he rode on, his first meal in three days lying heavily undigested in his stomach.

Two more days. Two more days of weary travel. And then at last he saw it lying before him, a cluster of buildings built at the edge of the long slope containing the seep that had given the town its name.

His horse traveled sluggishly now, his spirit gone and with it most of his strength. His head hung low, and occasionally he faltered. At the very edge of town, the horse stumbled and fell in the middle of the road.

Morgan Orr stepped clear as the horse fell. He looked at the dying animal with pity, then drew his gun and put a bullet into the horse's head. Returning the gun to its holster, he unbuckled the cinch and dragged his saddle clear.

He flung it to the ground and looked at it disgustedly. He turned and stared at the town. His mouth had a faintly bitter cast.

The homecoming of Morgan Orr. He made a rueful smile of self-mockery. He looked down at his ragged clothes, felt his stubbled face. He looked at the beat-up saddle, cracked and ruined by weather. He looked down at the smooth, worn, walnut grips of his gun.

Broke and hungry, hounded and defeated, sick of the past and all the memories stored in the past. Would it be any different here? Which Morgan Orr would the town remember—the boy it had pitied because of Sam Orr's drunken brutality? Or the gunfighter, whose name was legend, whose speed with a gun was the talk of a thousand frontier saloons?

Morgan's mouth twisted. Then with a small shrug, he picked up his saddle, flung it to his shoulder and trudged away toward the center of town.

The lack of change in the town was weird. Looking at it, Morgan could almost believe he had never been away. The shacks that clustered this upper end of Main seemed neither more shabby nor less so than when he had ridden out ten years before. The Antlers Hotel, at the Second Street intersection, still wore its cracked and peeling yellow paint. The Arapaho Wells bank, diagonally across from it, was still solid and unimaginative, still slept in the morning sun.

Halfway down the street he stopped. He stood for a moment, a puzzled frown on his face, wondering where he was bound, now that he was here, and what he would do. He hadn't the price of a meal, nor the price of a hotel room.

Aware, then, of the saddle's weight, he headed toward the livery barn.

An odd excitement possessed him as he walked. Did Tena Ward still live here? Would he see her on the street as he walked along?

His depression returned. He hoped not. Not this way. He didn't want her to see him, unshaven, ragged and beat. He began to hurry.

A few townspeople stared at him. A man rode in from the edge of town, passed Morgan with a long, appraising stare, then turned and headed down Second toward the sheriff's office. Probably to report the dead horse in the road at the edge of town, thought Morgan. It wouldn't be long. In another hour the word

6

that Morgan Orr had returned would be all over town. The women would pass it over their back fences. The men would hurry about town, talking of nothing else. Then Morgan would begin to feel the brunt of their disapproval.

They'd want him to leave. To them, he'd be like a bundle of dynamite sticks with a smoldering fuse. They'd want no violence in their town and they'd know that Morgan Orr would attract violence as a magnet attracts iron filings.

Only they'd be wrong. Morgan had had his fill of violence. Now, all he wanted was peace, a chance to work, a chance to forget.

He passed the Silver Dollar Saloon and the Buckhorn, across the street from it. Then he stepped through the livery stable archway and lowered his saddle to the ground.

Even this was unchanged. On one side was the tack-room, on the other a small office containing a dusty, roll-top desk and a potbellied stove.

Si Booth came from the office, a bridle he was mending still in his hands. He was older, thought Morgan. Grayer and a little more stooped. He peered at Morgan over the gold-rimmed glasses he wore pinched to his nose. 'Howdy, mister. What'll it be?'

Morgan realized that Si hadn't recognized him. He said, 'I want to sell this saddle.'

Si stooped and peered at the battered thing. He glanced up. 'Two dollars. Ain't wuth that.'

7

Morgan said, 'Sold.'

Booth stood up, looking at him curiously and nearsightedly. He fished a long pocketbook out of a side pocket, opened it and fumbled inside. He stepped closer to Morgan, peering up.

Recognition touched his face as he dropped two silver dollars into Morgan's hands. 'Morgan Orr!'

'That's right, Si.' This close, Morgan could smell the old man's sweaty, stable odor. He stooped to get his saddlebags, slicker and blanket, then stood up again.

Si looked him up and down. 'The gun ain't bought you much.'

Morgan's mouth twisted. 'Not much.' He suddenly wanted to get away. There was no pleasure in this. All at once he realized how little Si Booth had meant to him when he'd been here before, how little any of the town's inhabitants had meant to him. He'd never even bothered to be curious about them. He just hadn't cared.

And he realized, with shocking suddenness, that before people will care about a man, he first has to care about them.

An odd, strained silence had fallen between them. Morgan said, 'Thanks,' and turned to go.

Behind him Booth queried, 'Stayin', Morg?'

Morgan nodded without turning. He stepped out into the sunlight.

Passing the restaurant next to the Silver Dollar, he caught the smell of bacon frying, the indefinable accompanying odors that mean breakfast anywhere. He turned, stepped inside, and laid his gear beside the door.

A middle-aged woman Morgan didn't know was behind the counter. She said, 'Wash up in back. What'll it be?'

'Bacon. Eggs. Flapjacks.' He hesitated a moment, knowing his bridges were burning behind him. His horse was dead, his saddle sold. If he left, he'd walk. If they wouldn't let him stay.

He went around the counter and out the back door. He carefully scrubbed off the grime of the journey, dried on a dirty towel, and rubbing his whiskered face, went slowly back inside.

The woman brought him a steaming mug of coffee and he sipped it gratefully. It had been almost a month since he'd had any coffee. A month of running, of riding at night and hiding by day. A month of living off the country, and not living well.

He ate hungrily, almost weak from lack of food now that there was so much before him. The woman watched him curiously. 'You act like you hadn't et in quite a spell.'

He smiled at her, and the smile changed his face, took the hardness, the wariness from it. 'I haven't, and this is good.'

'Passin' through?'

9

He shook his head. 'I hope to stay. Know of any jobs?'

She frowned. 'Can't say I do. Wrong time of year to hunt a job.'

Morgan didn't reply. He finished his coffee and drew a long breath. 'How much?'

'Thirty-five. Usually it's twenty-five, but you et a heap.'

Morgan laid a dollar on the counter. 'Take out another nickel for a sack of Bull Durham.'

'That'll be forty, then.' She took the dollar, gave him his tobacco and change. Morgan sat at the counter while he rolled a smoke. He lighted it and drew the smoke deep into his lungs. Strength was beginning to flow back through his body. He felt he could face them now.

He went to the door, picked up his gear and stepped outside. He started toward the hotel.

A shrill voice shouted, 'There he is! That's Morgan Orr!'

Morgan felt a flush stain the back of his neck. He had hoped it wouldn't be like this. He hadn't even realized it was Saturday.

They converged from all sides. From the looks of them he thought every kid in town must be there. He hurried along, with the kids trailing at his heels, silent now with awe. He stifled the irritation he felt, but he didn't look around.

He tramped into the hotel, and a gruff voice on the veranda kept the kids outside. He

10

crossed the tiled lobby floor to the desk. This would not be easy, this staying here. He had a dollar and sixty cents to his name. He had to eat and he had to have a place to stay. He had to have a job.

He could see from the clerk's pale face that the man knew who he was. Morgan said, 'I want a room.'

'Sure, Mr Orr. Sure.' The clerk slid a key across the desk. 'Take number two at the head of the stairs. It'll be a dollar, and the boss says I got to have it in advance.'

'Osborne still own this place?'

'No sir. Osborne's dead. Mr Shank is the boss now.'

Morgan slid a dollar to the clerk. He turned and went up the stairs. He opened the door numbered two and stepped inside, closing the door behind. From habit, he locked it and pocketed the key.

He felt his body relax. He crossed to the bed and laid down on it. Its softness was like a sedative to his exhausted body.

But his mind wouldn't rest. How many towns had he entered like this? He didn't know. What he did know was that it never changed; it was always the same. Recognition came first— then fear as they wondered why he had come and what he was going to do.

He shivered slightly, but his mind kept working, kept drifting back, town by town and man by man, until it reached the first—the first

11

man to die under the gun of Morgan Orr.

That had been right here in Arapaho Wells, when he was twenty. Down at Si Booth's livery barn. Odd that remembrance of it should wait until now to come back to him. Strange that he hadn't remembered it as he stood in the stable talking to old man Booth.

Because it had changed his life.

He sat up irritably and made another cigarette. He'd been trying to leave town, trying to avoid a showdown with the stranger he'd gotten into an argument with in the Buckhorn the night before. Dan English, the sheriff, had broken it up and advised Morgan to leave until things cooled off.

He'd tried, too. But the stranger hadn't wanted it to end that way. He'd been waiting for Morgan as he stepped in the door at Booth's, a little after sunup.

Morgan still didn't know why he hadn't been killed. He'd been taken completely by surprise. Perhaps the man hadn't expected such speed and skill from a man as young as he. Whatever the reason, it ended with the stranger dead on the floor, with Morgan unhurt, a smoking gun in his hand.

He tried staying afterward, and he admitted now that it was mostly his own fault that he'd failed. He'd been defiant because the town criticized his action. And he wouldn't learn from the experience and put away his gun. Old man Daybright, out at Four-D, fired him that fall, although he'd always kept Morgan on before. And Morgan, bitter over that, rode out of town.

The following events fell into place naturally, with inevitable regularity. Straight riding jobs were scarce. But for a man with a gun there was always work. By the time Morgan saw where his life was leading, it was too late.

He got up, went to the window and stared down at the street. Occasionally someone passing in the street would glance up at the windows of the hotel.

Discouragement touched Morgan. He was notorious. He was known everywhere. There wasn't a town to which he could go without being recognized. And here it would be worse, because here was where he had been born and raised.

His mouth turned down at the corners. Raised wasn't exactly the word. Sam Orr hadn't been home enough during the years Morgan was growing to raise anything.

Morgan cooked for himself, washed for himself, kept house for himself. When Sam Orr did come home, he was usually drunk and mean. He took out his own anger at the world on Morgan with a quirt until that day when Morgan was sixteen.

That day he'd taken the quirt away from his father. He'd thrown it through the window. He'd meant to beat the old man with his fists,

13

but after the first blow he'd turned in disgust and run outside.

That wasn't the end. More years had followed—years of living under conditions of armed truce. He let Sam alone; Sam did the same with him.

Savagely he wished his mind would stop. He heard steps on the stairs outside his door, steps that halted in front of it. And then he heard a knock.

CHAPTER TWO

Instinct and long habit made him tense. Deliberately he relaxed himself and fumbled in his pocket for the key. He put it in the door, turned it, and stepped back. 'Come in.' He was thinking that a man never entirely puts away the past. This for instance. You let your visitor open the door instead of doing it yourself. Maybe it kept you alive.

The door swung open. Sam Orr stood in the hall.

Sight of him was a shock to Morgan. He said without expression, 'Come on in and shut the door.'

Sam Orr's face was as stubbled as Morgan's. Morgan turned his back and fumbled in his saddlebags for his razor. He crossed to the dresser and dumped water from the pitcher

14

into the basin. He lathered and began to shave.

Sam said with sour disapproval, 'You ain't changed.'

Morgan looked around. He didn't know what he'd expected of his father. Maybe he hadn't even thought about it. He said, 'Neither have you.'

It wasn't true. Sam had changed. He was older. The lines of his face were deeper, uglier. His eyes were red and evil. There was a little drool of saliva at one corner of his mouth. Morgan knew it was wrong to hate Sam, but he couldn't help it.

Sam had been drinking, not an unusual circumstance even at this hour. He said flatly, 'Get out of town. Stay out.'

Morgan held the razor poised and shook his head. 'Not this time. This time I'm going to stay. This is my home.'

Vindictive obscenity flooded from Sam's mouth. His face reddened. Morgan realized that his hands were clenched and shaking. He put the razor down.

He waited until Sam stopped for breath. Then he said, 'Get out of here. Get out before I finish what I started when I was sixteen.'

Sam opened his mouth to speak, but Morgan's eyes stopped him. He lowered his own glance and mumbled, 'I ain't afraid of you. You and your big name! You wouldn't dare kill your own pa.'

Morgan unbuckled his gunbelt and tossed it

15

on the bed. He took a step toward Sam.

Sam Orr turned and fled. He slammed the door behind him and stumbled down the hall toward the stairs.

A feeling of nausea was in Morgan's stomach, the same feeling of nausea he'd known so many times as a boy. It was compounded of fear, and disgust, and perhaps hurt, too, he realized now. He realized something else as well, for the first time. Sam wasn't worth it.

He finished shaving and toweled his face. He strapped on his gun and went out the door.

There were two men and a woman in the lobby. One of the men stared at him with open curiosity. The other watched him furtively over the top of a newspaper. The woman's face flushed, as though with outrage or anger at his very presence.

Morgan strode outside. Lord, you'd think he'd get used to the way people looked at him after a while. But he never had.

He turned the corner and headed, walking fast, toward the sheriff's office. The kids watched him from their places of concealment and when he had gone by, fell in a safe distance behind in worshipful, silent awe.

Morgan's mouth twisted. He was a hero to the kids, a murdering son of a bitch to the grownups. Two extremes, neither of which he liked. Why couldn't there be something in between? Why couldn't he be just a person—a

16

human being like everyone else?

With a rare burst of insight, he realized suddenly that it was a right he'd have to earn.

An odd sense of uneasiness troubled him before he had gone a dozen steps from the intersection. He glanced around warily, and his eyes fixed themselves on a man standing before the bank. The man was watching him with a peculiarly intent look on his face.

Morgan let his eyes rest on the man briefly. He didn't recognize him, and assumed the man had come to Arapaho Wells in the ten years since he'd been gone.

He was a big man, in a conservative business suit. He wore no hat, so he had probably just stepped from the bank. It was likely that he worked there.

This Morgan's glance told him, and then he turned away. But his puzzlement at the peculiar intensity of the man's glance remained. Did the man know him from somewhere? He shook his head. He had never forgotten a face. He was sure he'd never seen the man before in his life.

The sheriff's office was a sandstone-block building, dun in color, with bars at the windows. The rear of the building housed the jail.

The sheriff, Dan English, sat on a bench outside the door in the shade, reading a newspaper. He watched Morgan over the top of it as he approached.

17

When Morgan was ten feet away, he lowered the paper and folded it carefully. 'Hello, Morgan. I heard you were in town.'

A neutral voice, neither hostile nor friendly. Dan English was a man of medium height, stockily built and beginning to grow a slight paunch. He was forty-five years old.

Morgan said, 'I want to talk to you. Can we go inside?'

English stood up. Morgan looked back up Second Street toward Main. The man he had noticed was still standing before the bank.

Morgan asked, 'Who's that, Dan?'

'Who?'

'Up in front of the bank.'

English glanced that way. He said, 'Mel Jerome, the banker.' His tone was clipped and short. He went in the door and Morgan followed. He turned and looked closely at Morgan, but when Morgan's glance met his, he looked away. He said, 'You ain't here to make trouble, are you?'

Morgan said, 'I'm here to stay. And I need a job.'

Dan English stared, and then he frowned. 'Gun job?'

'No, just a job. Any kind of a job.'

English looked at him suspiciously. 'What do you really want, Morg? What are you here for? Why all that interest in Mel Jerome?'

Morgan fished in his pocket. His hand came out with a half dollar and a dime. 'This is what

18

ten years of gun jobs have got me. Sixty cents, a dead horse in the middle of the road, and a worn-out gun. Now do you believe I want a change?'

English's scowl deepened. He studied the toe of his boot. He said, 'That's something I wanted to see you about. That horse. It cost the county three dollars to get it dragged away.'

'I'll owe it to you, Dan.'

English shrugged. 'I'll pay it for old times sake, if you'll leave town.'

'How? Walking?'

English shrugged. He refused to lift his eyes from the toe of his boot. Morgan said evenly, controlling his temper with difficulty, 'I need a job, Dan. An honest job. I came to you to see if you knew...'

'I don't. It's gettin' on toward winter. There ain't no jobs.'

Temper stirred Morgan. 'And if there were, you wouldn't tell me about them. Is that it?'

The sheriff looked at him defiantly. 'What if it is? Do you blame me, Morg? You're trouble for any town. I don't want you here and neither does anybody else.'

'That's plain enough.' There was both anger and resentment in Morgan, but there was reluctant understanding too. No matter how hard Morgan Orr tried to stay out of trouble, it wouldn't work. It never had—not since his name had become well known. There was always somebody, in every community, that didn't think he was as good as he was cracked up to be and tried to find out.

He shrugged. 'I'll manage without you. But I've got to stay. Can't you understand that, Dan? This is my last chance to live like other people do.'

Dan's face didn't soften. Morgan stared into it a moment, then turned and went outside.

He wanted desperately to ask Dan English about Tena, but he knew it wouldn't be right. Rumors started fast enough without him starting them. He'd have to wait.

He walked slowly up toward Main. He turned right toward the Buckhorn. A beer. Maybe two. Enough for dinner in midafternoon. A place to sleep tonight. And that was it.

But he might see someone in the Buckhorn he could ask for a job.

Walking, he wondered what it was about being broke and needing a job that made a man feel like a beggar. Morgan Orr wasn't used to feeling like that. His kind of services had been in demand now for ten long years. Men who wanted him came to him. They talked to him respectfully. They called him Mr Orr.

Something made him turn his head. He saw Mel Jerome, the banker, cross the street and head down Second, hurrying, without his hat. As Jerome passed out of sight, he turned his head and glanced at Morgan.

Morgan frowned. He was used to being

20

stared at. He was used to dislike, fear, even awe. But something about the way Mel Jerome looked at him bothered him, because it seemed to be more personally concerned than the other looks he got.

Frowning slightly, he stepped into the Buckhorn Saloon.

*   *   *

Mel Jerome slammed into the sheriff's office and closed the door behind him. His face was white, and there was a film of sweat on his wide, heavy brow. He looked toward the rear of the building, and asked almost breathlessly, 'Anybody back there, Dan?'

'No. What the hell's eatin' you?' Dan English stared at Jerome with open dislike.

'Morgan Orr. What else?'

'Why?' A frown of puzzlement crossed the sheriff's face.

'Why? For God's sake, Dan, maybe he was sent to check up on that damned bank examiner.'

English stared hard at Jerome. His voice was soft, but it was filled with quiet anger. 'God damn you, Jerome, I hope he was. I hope he finds out who killed that examiner and where his body is hidden. I hope he exposes the whole dirty mess.'

Some of the whiteness left Jerome's face. His eyes glittered with anger. 'You're in it as deep

21

as I am, Dan. You better not hope that.'

Dan English met Jerome's eyes steadily, with mounting dislike. He said evenly, 'Maybe I am in it now. But only for one reason. I like this town. I like the people in it. I owe them a lot. I didn't keep still about Rossiter because of you and the Grego brothers. I kept still because I knew if the people in Arapaho Wells realized the bank was broke they'd start a run on it. And if they did, they'd all be ruined. This way, maybe you can get the bank back on its feet. If you don't, God help me, I'll kill you myself. Now get back up the street to your bank. I don't want to look at you. I don't even want to think about you.'

Jerome flinched. Then his eyes began to burn.

He was big, broad-shouldered, looking more like a section hand than a banker, and indeed he had been a section hand for several years when he was younger.

Dan English knew a little about him. He knew that Jerome had lived on a Kansas homestead in abject poverty that included actual hunger until he reached sixteen and ran away. He knew that in Jerome, as in many men with similar backgrounds, success financially was a burning, consuming need that couldn't be denied.

Only Jerome had tried to hasten it. Eventually he'd have made it big with just the Arapaho Wells bank. Instead, he'd used the bank's assets to speculate in mining properties over in Oro City and Cripple Creek. And he'd lost his shirt.

Six months ago, Rossiter, a state bank examiner, came in on the eastbound stage. He found everything he needed in the first day he spent in the bank.

That night, Rossiter, a dry little man, left the hotel to take a walk in the warm Spring air. He never returned. He disappeared.

Bill Shank, the hotel proprietor called Dan English in the next day. Dan had conducted a quiet investigation that ended up with Mel Jerome at the bank. Jerome was a frightened man and it showed. Under Dan's careful questioning he tripped on his own garbled story and eventually broke down.

Dan scowled. He repeated, 'Get out of here. Go on back to your bank.'

Jerome went outside. He glanced up Second Street, his eyes dilated with fear.

Dan watched him until he went in the door of the bank. Maybe he should have reassured Jerome. Dan knew Morgan Orr wasn't an investigator. He should have convinced Jerome that he wasn't. No telling what the banker would do.

A spare smile touched the sheriff's mouth. Tackling Morgan Orr would be different than tackling a dry little bank examiner. Jerome would find that out.

Morgan stepped into the Buckhorn and crossed to the bar. At this time of morning, the place was quiet. A swamper was sweeping the floor. Len Smith, the bartender, was polishing glasses. Two men stood at the bar, another sat at one of the tables reading a Denver newspaper, the Rocky Mountain News.

Morgan said, 'A beer, Len,' and slid out a dime.

Len drew the beer without speaking, raked off the head with a polished stick, then slid the glass to Morgan. It stopped precisely in front of him. Len said, 'Heard you were back, Morg. How long you goin' to stay?'

'For good.' Morgan raised the beer and drank, then wiped the foam from his mouth with the back of his hand.

The other two at the bar turned to look at him. He recognized one of them. The other was a stranger.

The one he knew was Chuck Grego. Grego was a man slightly shorter than Morgan. He wore denim jeans that were shiny with grease, a sweat-stained khaki shirt and a ragged vest from the pocket of which dangled a Bull Durham tag. His hat was black, shapeless, and stained with sweat and dust immediately above the band. His boots were scuffed and run down at the heels. He wore big Spanish cartwheel spurs.

His face was unshaven, and the seams of it were black with dirt. His eyes were bright as a weasel's.

He spat a stream of tobacco juice at the brass cuspidor and wiped his mouth. When he spoke it was around the cud he held in his cheek. 'Heard you were back, Morg. Whadda ya goin' to do? Ain't much work for a man of your talents around Arapaho Wells.'

Even at a distance of ten feet, Morgan could smell him. He wondered if Grego ever took a bath, or even washed his face. Grego was grinning at him, and his teeth were almost black. Morgan said, 'I'm hunting a job.'

Grego cackled. Morgan looked at him steadily, and the cackle died. Grego looked away, and finished his beer.

A young man with horn-rimmed glasses came in the door, looked around briefly, then crossed to Grego. He said something to Chuck in a low voice. Grego nodded and left the saloon with the man.

Morgan nodded to Smith. 'Another.' Bleak discouragement was beginning to creep over him. If time hadn't been so short, perhaps it wouldn't have bothered him so soon. But he had today, and tonight, and that was all.

The door banged open and a young man came in.

He was taller than Morgan, and weighed about ten pounds more. A good-looking kid of about nineteen, he wore his gun as Morgan did, low on his right thigh. The bottom of the holster was tied above his knee with a rawhide thong.

Something was vaguely familiar about him, but recognition didn't come until the bartender said, 'What'll you have, Roy?'

Roy Forette. Morgan remembered him now. The reason he hadn't before was that Roy had been only nine when Morgan left.

Forette came up beside Morgan, and looked at him with an admiring half grin. 'You haven't changed much.'

Morgan grinned wryly. 'What did you expect, horns and a tail?'

'Maybe. You've made a name.'

Morgan grunted.

Enthusiasm sparkled in Forette's eyes. 'What's it like? What's it like to ride into a town and cause an uproar like you have here?'

Morgan stared at him sourly. 'I walked into this town.'

Forette hitched at his gun, then flushed faintly. Looking at him, Morgan could see himself ten years before. It was almost like looking into a mirror. He said, 'Take a look at me. A good look.' He finished his beer disgustedly.

Morgan turned and stalked to the door. He was tired of talk about himself, his gun, his reputation, the last ten years of his life. Yet that seemed to be all anyone wanted to talk to him about.

He banged out the door, and stood a

moment in the autumn sun, making a smoke. He saw Chuck Grego, come out of the bank, glance downstreet at him, then mount up and gallop out of town.

He remembered the young man who had come after Grego. A bareheaded, pale young man in a business suit.

An employee of the bank. Jerome had sent him for Grego. That was obvious.

He shook his head impatiently. It didn't matter. It didn't concern him.

He walked back to the hotel, crossed the lobby and climbed the stairs to his room. The door was slightly ajar.

At once tension came to him, an old thing that was part of his overdeveloped instinct of self-preservation. Deliberately, he put it away from him. The last ten years were past. He had to start living like other men sometime and it might as well begin now.

He pushed the door open and stepped into the room. When he saw his visitor, he closed it quickly behind him.

She had been standing at the window, looking into the street. Now she turned.

For a long moment their glances locked. Neither spoke. Tena reminded him of a frightened girl, who would like to run but cannot.

Then, slowly, her glance left his face and took in his clothes. It returned to his face, searching. Her eyes brightened briefly with tears of compassion. She said softly, 'Hello, Morgan.'

She was dressed in a dark brown gown of rustling silk. At her throat and wrists were ruffles of snowy lace. A tiny, ridiculous hat perched atop her darkly shining hair.

He had not remembered her as being quite this small. Perhaps the strength in her had put into his memory an impression of more size.

Morgan took off his hat and sailed it onto the bed. He ran his fingers through his sweat-damp hair. It had been six years since he'd seen her and six years was a long time.

He wanted to touch her, and wanting that, remembrance of that night six years before came flooding to his mind. He said, 'You're looking well, Tena.'

'Thank you, Morgan.' Awkwardness was between them, but there was the old undercurrent of closeness too.

He said, 'Sit down,' and gestured toward the bed.

She crossed to the bed and sat down on the edge of it, her eyes never leaving his face. Morgan got a straight-backed chair and straddled it, resting his arms on its back.

For a long moment neither spoke. The silence grew long and heavy. When they did speak, both spoke at once, then stopped and laughed self-consciously. Morgan murmured, 'Go ahead. What were you going to say?'

'I was going to ask why you'd come back,

Morgan.'

'Does it matter?'

'It does to me, a great deal, Morgan. Because I'm married now.'

He glanced at the door uneasily. 'Then you shouldn't...'

Her voice was soothing. 'It's all right, Morgan. I came up the back way. Maria showed me your room.'

Morgan asked, 'Who is he?' A heaviness had come to his thoughts, and he was realizing, suddenly, that Tena had had more to do with his return than he had known.

'Mel Jerome. He owns the bank. He ... Morgan, I had to do something. After you were here ... well ...' Her eyes suddenly met his beseechingly. 'I found out I was going to have your child.'

For an instant Morgan felt stunned. He stared at her with stupid surprise, and saw something in her face he had not seen before. Unhappiness. Confusion.

He started to get up and Tena flinched. 'No Morgan. Please.'

He settled back, his hands clenched. More than anything else in the world he wanted to take her in his arms. But he couldn't.

She talked rapidly then, as though she had to get said what she needed to say before she broke down. 'I didn't know what to do, Morgan. I didn't know where you were. I couldn't bear to have our child born without a

29

name. I knew it wasn't fair to Mel to let him think ... but ...'

'He thinks it's his?'

She nodded dumbly. 'I've tried to make it up to him. I've tried to be a good wife.' Her voice firmed with determination, 'And I'll go on trying, Morgan. I'll go on ...' Her voice caught. Tears flooded from her eyes. She fought them visibly, then wiped her cheeks and eyes with a tiny scrap of a handkerchief.

Morgan clenched his jaws. His hands on the chairback were knuckle-white.

More composedly, Tena repeated, 'Why did you come back, Morgan? You can't stay. Please don't stay. I can't ... Oh Morgan, why? Why, after all these years?'

'I had to. I had to, Tena. I couldn't run anymore.'

'Run?'

'It's what I've been doing, for nearly a year. Running because if I stayed and fought I'd kill again. And again. I'm tired of it, Tena. I never pass a lighted house but what ... Oh hell!' He shook his head helplessly. 'I just want to live like other men, not like some kind of wild animal that has to fight at every turn.'

Tena got up nervously and went to the window. Her hands worked savagely at the handkerchief, until it was shredded. Her face was white, her eyes miserable when she turned. 'Then stay, Morgan,' she whispered. 'Stay no matter what anyone says.'

He felt his throat tightening. 'What is it, Tena—a boy or a girl?'

'A girl. Her name is Serena. She's five years old.'

'Could I...'

'See her? Of course, Morgan. I'm going home now. I'll bring her past here...' She shook her head with helpless shame. 'That isn't fair. You ought to be able to hold her. You ought...'

Morgan's face was hard. 'No.' He swallowed, and then said, 'Just walk her by the hotel ... Just walk her by.'

Tena nodded dumbly. She walked to the door, hesitated with her hand on the knob. She turned her head and looked at him, her eyes brimming. 'I'm sorry, Morgan. Oh God, I'm sorry!' And then she went out, closing the door firmly behind her.

CHAPTER THREE

Morgan crossed to the window and stared into the street. After a while he saw Tena turn the corner from Second Street and cross to the other side of Main. She glanced up at his window as she passed, then looked quickly away.

He followed her trim, straight figure all the way up the block until she disappeared from sight as she turned the corner onto Third.

He could not have been shocked more by anything than to be told he had a daughter five years old. Yet now, his mind was recovering from that shock, and he caught himself watching the corner of Third and Main with more intentness than he had ever watched a man he knew he had to fight.

He thought of how it must have been for Tena, discovering she was going to have a child, being all alone. He was suddenly deeply shamed. He should have stayed. Six years ago would not have been too late. Six years ago he could have stopped.

Now it *was* too late. He remembered the way Roy Forette had watched him down in the Buckhorn. He'd known what had been going on in Forette's mind. He'd seen that look too often before to miss its significance. Forette had been thinking that the man who killed Morgan Orr would have his reputation made. There would be no long, hard road to the top. He'd have gained the top.

The idea would eat on Forette's mind. Maybe it would take him several days to work his courage up to the necessary pitch. But when he had, he'd make his play.

And what would Morgan do when he did? He shook his head. He didn't know. What he did know was that if he killed Forette, he couldn't stay in Arapaho Wells. He'd have to go on—drifting—from one gunfight to the next until he reached the last—the one he couldn't win.

Forcibly he tore his mind from Forette. He made himself think of Tena—of that night six years before.

He'd been nearly exhausted when he knocked on her door. It had been late— midnight or after. Morgan had thought he had two brothers on his trail, who'd followed him from Albuquerque trying to avenge the death of a third, a third that Morgan Orr had killed, in self defense. What he didn't know was that they'd given up the chase at the top of Raton Pass.

There had always been something between Morgan and Tena Ward. Closeness. Understanding. Friendship. It was natural for Morgan to turn to her, the one person he trusted, for help.

Oh God, if he'd only known! If he'd only known there was no pursuit. He could have stayed then because his reputation was not so big, not so widely known.

They had talked, that night, for hours it seemed. And as they talked an awareness of each other crept into their thoughts and words until nothing could have kept them apart. Thinking of it, Morgan's blood beat hot and fast.

Then, suddenly, all thought was driven from him. Around the corner of Main and Third came Tena, a little girl beside her holding her hand.

Tena's eyes were on his window almost until she came abreast. Then she looked straight ahead, her face pale, her body proud and straight.

Morgan felt tears burning behind his eyes. His throat was nearly closed.

He had to have them—both Tena and his daughter. They went into the bank, and Morgan whirled toward the door.

He stopped in mid-stride. It was Jerome, not Morgan, whose name Serena bore. Jerome, not Morgan had assumed the responsibilities of husband and father. Morgan could not now claim that which he had left unclaimed these many years.

He sat down on the bed and dropped his head into his hands. He sat there motionless for a time, then stood up and began to pace the floor.

He remembered the unhappiness and confusion that had been in Tena's eyes. He felt his anger against Jerome begin to rise.

A burst of honesty within himself stopped him. He wouldn't have made Tena any happier. He couldn't honestly say that with him she would have been completely happy. And what could he offer them now? A man whose only means of support was his gun. A man who was considered wild game by most of the inhabitants of the land, like a predator that ought to be killed.

Anger and tension, born of frustration and

helplessness, began to grow in him. He drew his gun and held it in his palm while he looked at it with brooding eyes.

The walnut grips were worn smooth. The blue was worn from the barrel and cylinder by countless draws. A smooth, oiled piece of precision whose only purpose was death.

He jammed it angrily back into his holster, knowing that as long as he carried it, he would be only halfhearted about his determination to stay and build his life anew. If he put it away, here in his room, the thought would always be with him that it lay, a few steps from him, ready for whatever might arise.

Yet if he sold it, he'd be strictly on his own. No longer would the gun serve him as a crutch, to lean upon when the going got too tough. Without the gun he would have to stand or fall on his own.

A gunman without a gun. Target for every glory hound that came through town. Unarmed, he might be killed tonight— tomorrow—on any day at any time. The country was full of people who hated him— with reason or without.

He strode to the window and looked down. People passed and repassed in the street below. Tena and her daughter came from the bank and walked toward home. Tena glanced up once, her face white with strain.

Decision came hard to Morgan. But it came, at last. Getting rid of the gun was the only expression of good faith the town would understand. If he wanted to stay there was nothing else that he could do.

* * *

Tena Jerome's face was troubled as she left the bank. Her eyes were hurt and puzzled.

Little Serena, holding tightly to her hand, walked along for almost a block before she looked up and asked, 'Why was Daddy so mad, mama?'

Tena had been puzzling the same question. She said in a preoccupied way, 'I don't know, dear. Something about the bank, I suppose.'

She wondered if the bank were in trouble. She tried, in her mind, to decide when this change had begun in her husband. She shook her head confusedly. It had been sometime during the past year. He'd begun taking trips over to the mining camps in the mountains last fall, saying he had business interests there. But the real trouble had begun about six months ago.

Tena recalled suddenly that about six months ago Rossiter, the bank examiner, had come to town. And disappeared.

A small chill ran down Tena's spine. No! She wouldn't believe that!

She hated herself suddenly, hated the way her mind was working. She gazed inward, honestly, and admitted that she still loved

36

Morgan Orr.

Not particularly proud of her feelings, she rationalized that because she still loved Morgan, she was trying to justify herself by destroying Mel. She had actually suspected him for a moment there of being involved in Rossiter's disappearance.

She reached her house, a big, white, two-story building surrounded by enormous cottonwoods. There was a big lawn in front of the house. Serena pulled her hand loose and ran to play.

From the kitchen came the sounds of banging pans as Sophronia, her Indian cook, prepared the noonday meal. Small and nervous, Tena paced the floor of the parlor, glancing out occasionally at Serena playing on the lawn.

In her mind was an image, one that wouldn't go away. It was of a man, tall, slender, muscular, clad in trail-worn clothes, a gun nestling snugly against his thigh as though it had grown there.

It was his eyes she would never forget—not as long as she lived. Haunted eyes—hungry eyes—eyes that looked bleakly along the trail ahead and saw nothing but loneliness and ultimate disaster.

Tears ran across Tena's smooth cheeks. Because she was helpless to ease that haunted look. She could do nothing but watch, while the town showed Morgan the edge of its hostility and eventually drove him out.

He must have known that they wouldn't accept him. In his heart he must have known. Only pure desperation could have let him convince himself they would. Only a man who was lost could even have tried to come back and stay.

Her small hands clenched helplessly, Tena wondered what he had felt, what he had thought, as he saw Serena walking along beside her. How would it have changed her life, and Serena's, if Morgan had known sooner? Could he have changed six years ago?

She didn't know. Her face grew anguished, as her mind and thoughts went back. She remembered that night six years ago, and Morgan, exhausted, standing at her door.

She would never forget that night—the electric touch of his hand—the intolerable ecstasy of lying in his arms.

Her face grew hot. This wasn't fair to Mel. It wasn't fair at all. But there'd been nothing shameful about that night—not in Tena's mind. Because she'd loved Morgan for a long, long time. She'd never stopped, even though he went away, even though she was convinced she'd never see him again.

Now she had his child. If she never had anything more than that, she had his child.

CHAPTER FOUR

Morgan went down the stairs thoughtfully and a little regretfully, too. Out in the street, he walked along, ignoring the attention he received from the passers-by, until, near the Silver Dollar, he saw a gunsmith's shop.

It had not been here when he'd left. Nor did he know the balding man inside. Apparently, however, the man knew him. At the sound of the bell attached to the door, he came hustling out from the back room, tripped over a footstool and almost fell, then recovered self-consciously. 'Mornin', Mr Orr. What can I do for you?' He laughed uneasily. 'Bet you know more about guns than a gunsmith does.'

Morgan unbuckled his gunbelt and laid his holstered gun and belt on the counter. 'I want to sell this. Are you interested in buying it?'

'Am I? Good Lord, Mr Orr...' A shrewd look crossed the man's face, but it didn't restrain the enthusiasm in his eyes. 'I'll give you a hundred dollars. Why if I ever wanted to, I could sell it for twice that.' His voice was an awed whisper. 'The gun of Morgan Orr!'

Disgust touched Morgan. He said evenly, 'Let's go back and start over. I want exactly what it's worth as a gun, not as a souvenir. The new price is only eighteen dollars.'

The gunsmith swallowed. His voice was a

whisper. 'Would fifteen dollars do?'

'Fair enough.'

The man counted out the money with shaking hands. When he had finished, he touched the gun reverently.

Sudden anger possessed Morgan. He controlled it with difficulty. It was anger, not only at the gunsmith, but at himself as well. Pride had dictated his refusal of the man's first offer. Foolish, stubborn pride. He didn't want to start his new life with proceeds from the old. It was that simple. Still, he knew the new life would have had a better chance on a hundred dollars than it would have on fifteen.

He walked out, closing the door firmly behind him as though closing a door on his past.

The money, in silver dollars, was a heavy weight in his pocket. He walked down to the stable first. He'd ride out to some of the ranches on a hired livery stable horse. There had to be one that needed a man. Besides the gun, cow work was all he knew.

Si Booth was sitting on a chopping block out in front of the livery, mending harness with an awl, beeswax and a spool of linen twine. Morgan stopped beside him and fished automatically for his Bull Durham sack. Si eyed the shiny place on Morgan's thigh where the gun had rubbed.

Morgan said, 'I need a horse.'

Si said, 'Dollar a day. And don't bring him

back hot.' He got up and ambled stiffly into the stable. Morgan heard him talking to one of the horses, heard the slap of the saddle hitting the horse's back. A moment later, Si came out with the horse, a chunky bay.

There was a strange expression in Si Booth's eyes, an expression both watchful and speculating. Morgan swung up and Si said, 'Good luck. I didn't know whether you meant what you said about stayin' or not, but it kind of looks like you did.'

Morgan said, 'I meant it.'

'It ain't goin' to be easy.'

'Didn't figure it would.' He rode away, down Main and across the dump at its foot. The horse picked his way daintily through the litter of rusted tin cans and broken bottles.

Once through the dump, Morgan eased up on the reins and the horse's gait moved into an easy canter. Morgan pointed him toward the Four-D outfit, where he'd worked ten years before, not even knowing whether old man Daybright was still alive.

The plain was rolling. Brown, belly-high grass waved in the breeze. In the distance, Morgan could see the escarpment of Rattlesnake Ridge, at the foot of which the Four-D ranch house stood.

He felt undressed without his gun, strangely defenseless and vulnerable. In spite of this, he felt a peacefulness at being home. Every landmark was as familiar to him as the palm of his own hand.

And yet, deep within him was a crawling uneasiness. He was like a wolf without teeth—like an old range bull without horns. If the inhabitants of this country would let him be, he'd be all right. If they wouldn't—and he knew they wouldn't—he was in for trouble.

Strange the compulsion people had to destroy a thing they feared. But Morgan had seen the compulsion at work too many times to doubt its existence now. Still, if he could get a job...

* * *

At noon, he rode into the yard of Four-D. The dinner triangle was clanging, but his pride wouldn't let him head for the cookshack first. Instead, he rode to the wide, long porch that was overgrown with morning glory vines, swung down and tied his horse. An old man was rocking on the porch, and it was several moments before Morgan recognized him as Rufus Daybright.

At the foot of the steps he stopped. 'Remember me, Mr Daybright?'

The old man's knees were covered with a blanket. His hands were gnarled and twisted with rheumatism. He needed a shave, and his face was gaunt. But his eyes were rational and bright. 'I sure as hell do, Morg.' He raised his voice and bawled, 'Luke! Joe! Come 'ere!'

A moment passed. Then the door to the cookshack banged open and two men crossed the yard.

They came up behind Morgan, one on each side, watchful, silent men with guns at their thighs. Old Rufus said, 'Now we can talk. What the hell do you want, Morgan?'

Morgan smiled thinly. 'Do you need a couple of guns around before you'll let a man ask you for a job?'

'If it's you that's askin', yes. I've heard about you, Morg. Everybody has. You're a killer—a goddam mean one. Gunfighter! Hah!' The old man snorted contemptuously. 'A word. Just a word to make killin' legal. Thing I want to know is why the hell you want a job with me. I don't want nobody killed.'

'I want a riding job. Like I had before.' Morgan's temper was wearing thin. He tried to keep the fact that it was out of his eyes.

'So you can hide out for a while. That it?'

'Nobody's on my trail.'

'Lost 'em, huh? But how long'll it be 'fore they pick it up again? How long, 'fore the word goes out you're hidin' on Four-D? Then the vultures'll begin to gather. All them as hates you. No sir. You haul your freight. I don't want your kind around here. Not ever!'

Behind Morgan a man said, 'You heard him. Git!'

Morgan swung and put his eyes on the man that had spoken. The man's hand went to his

43

gun and fell away. Morgan said, 'I'm unarmed. But don't try pushing.'

Without looking at Rufus Daybright again, he turned and stepped away. He headed directly at the man who had spoken to him, his eyes level and steady. The man stepped aside, then flushed because he had. He muttered something and Morgan turned his head. 'What?'

The man grumbled, 'Nothin'.'

Morgan untied his horse and swung astride. He turned and rode away. With the exception of Tena and Si Booth, he had encountered nothing but hostility from those who knew or recognized him.

He headed directly toward Rattlesnake Ridge, and when he reached its foot, turned right and continued for more than an hour until he hit a road winding back and forth to its top.

He turned his horse into the road and followed it over the ridge and down into a cluster of ranch buildings that nestled on the other side. This was Spear, the only other ranch in the country with enough size to possibly warrant keeping men through the winter.

He rode into the yard. Jess Spear, a scrawny, bow-legged man of about fifty-five, was replacing a pair of rusted hinges on a barn door. He had the door on saw-horses. Jess's wife, as scrawny as he, was hanging clothes on a line behind the house. A lone dog came out and barked at Morgan, and chickens scattered as he rode through them.

He rode up to Jess and sat his saddle looking down. 'Hello, Jess.'

Jess had watched him approach. Now his eyes clung to the shiny place on Morgan's right thigh. He raised his glance to meet Morgan's, and there was the same wariness in his eyes, the same veiled hostility Morgan had seen in everybody else.

Morgan said, 'A man changes, Jess. The years do that. I'm not packing a gun and I want a riding job.' It was as close as he could come to apology, as close as he'd ever come to pleading.

Jess laid down his hammer and fished for tobacco. For an instant, his grayish eyes were almost friendly, but only for an instant. Then he said, 'I'm letting men go. I do every winter.'

Morgan's eyes hardened. He nodded bleakly.

Jess said, 'Wait a minute. No call to get sore at me. Look at it from where I stand. I hire you and what's Daybright goin' to say? That I've got my eye on his grass or I wouldn't have hired a gun. The rest of my neighbors would see it the same way.'

Morgan nodded without speaking. Jess, ever a garrulous man, went on, warming up to his subject. 'You say you've changed. Well it takes more than sayin'. It takes doin'. Puts me in mind of a wolf cub I caught once. I raised it like

45

one of the dogs. It was tame, too, tame for a wolf anyhow. But you don't change the nature of 'em. When that pup got old enough it went out and joined a pack. It led them here and they cleaned out every chicken and turkey on the place in ten minutes.'

Morgan said evenly, 'You comparing me to that wolf pup?'

Jess got a little pale, but his eyes met Morgan's defiantly. 'Well, I reckon I was. You're wild, Morg. You got a mad against the world on account of your old man and all the things that've happened since. Goin' to be a spell before folks believe you when you say you've changed. You're goin' to have to show 'em.'

Morgan felt anger rising in him. He said sourly, 'How does a man show them? What's he eat while he's doing it? Nothing but crow?'

Jess didn't answer. He picked up his hammer.

Morgan shrugged. 'All right, Jess,' he said, and turned. He rode out of the yard slowly, conscious of Jess's glance on his back.

Discouragement was like lead in his body. He'd tried the two biggest ranches in the country, the only ones he knew who kept a crew on in winter. He'd been firmly refused both places.

If he'd had an outfit, he could have put the winter in catching wild horses over in the Red Butte country fifty miles away. But he hadn't

46

an outfit and pride wouldn't let him ask anyone to stake him. Not that anyone would.

Maybe they were right, he thought bleakly. Maybe a man couldn't change. Maybe when he killed his first man he doomed himself to live by the gun until he died.

He had the feeling he was being pushed and he didn't like it. Damn them, they weren't going to chart the course of his life for him. He'd do that himself. He'd do it if it killed him.

He rode slowly back toward town, somehow dreading his arrival there, wondering at the odd feeling of tension that was beginning to grip his mind and body. It was as though he sensed the approach of danger, and trouble, as an animal senses it. From out of nowhere came remembrance of Mel Jerome, of the strange way the man had stared at him. He recalled Chuck Grego, his summons from the bank, and his riding out of town. The tension that gripped him increased.

The simile Jess had used about the wolf clung in his mind. He'd seen a wolf pack once in midwinter on the high Montana plains— had seen them pull down and kill one of their own number.

Some strange impulse he hadn't understood himself had made him drive them off, killing several in the doing. The same strange impulse had made him dismount and examine the one they had killed.

It had been an old dog wolf, with most of his

teeth gone. Gaunt and starving and near to death.

Now there was a simile that fitted, and fitted well. Morgan was the old dog wolf; the people of Arapaho Wells were the pack. When Morgan took off his gun, he became like a wolf without his teeth ...

He shook himself visibly, as though he were trying to shake off his morbid thoughts. He rode slowly, toward town, and arrived in late afternoon.

The sun hung low and red above the western plain. He stared at the town and his eyes took in the numerous buggies, buckboards and racked horses along Main.

A Saturday night crowd. Normal. Or was it? Morgan remembered Saturday night in Arapaho Wells from ten years back, and it didn't seem there had ever been this big a crowd.

He rode through the stable archway and swung to the ground. Si Booth came out of his office. Morgan handed him the reins of the horse and a silver dollar.

Si asked, 'Do any good?'

Morgan shook his head. 'I tried Four-D and Spear. Can you think of anyone else that might use a man in winter?'

Si shook his head. He studied Morgan carefully. 'You said you didn't expect it to be easy.'

Morgan scowled at him. Slowly the scowl

48

faded and at last he grinned. 'That's what I said.'

Si watched him turn away, and called softly after him. 'It won't get any easier. You notice the crowd in town?'

Morgan swung his head. Si said, 'Maybe you ought to put that gun back on.'

'I sold it.'

'I could loan you one.'

Morgan walked back to him. 'You're trying to say something, Si. Say it.'

'The Grego brothers are in town, all three of 'em. They're talking, and they've got some of the others talking too.'

Morgan's voice was soft. 'What are they saying, Si?'

'That you ain't changed a damn bit. That you don't intend to give up the gun and stay. That you've got some other reason for bein' here and if the town knows what's good for it, they'll ride you out on a rail.'

Morgan said, 'Thanks, Si.' His eyes were glittering, his mouth hard. He stalked through the stable archway and out into the street. Si called after him, 'Better take that gun, Morg. Just havin' it will keep 'em off your back.'

Morgan didn't reply and he didn't look back. He walked along the worn boardwalk to the Buckhorn and stepped inside.

CHAPTER FIVE

Chuck Grego returned to Arapaho Wells in midafternoon while Morgan was out at Spear. He went directly to the bank, riding a little ahead of his two brothers. He dismounted and tied, and his brothers tied on either side of him.

Without speaking, Chuck led the way into the bank. The young man who had come to the Buckhorn after him earlier in the day said, 'He's expecting you. Go on back.' There was the faintest expression of distaste on the young man's face.

Chuck went through the swinging gate and back to Mel Jerome's office in the rear. He opened the door without knocking, waited beside it until his brothers were inside, then closed it again.

'All right. We're here. Now what?'

Jerome was obviously very nervous. He took a cigar out of his pocket, bit off the end, then lighted it with a hand that shook. 'He's here to check up on Rossiter. I know it.'

'You want him killed?'

'I don't know. If he's killed without reason they'll know there's something wrong.' Jerome studied Chuck. The first run of panic had slowed in him and he was beginning to think more clearly. He didn't like Chuck Grego, or Al, or Curt. Already their unwashed smell was beginning to fill the office. He didn't like the way their eyes watched him, either. He had a feeling they'd hold Rossiter over his head as long as he lived. Not that they weren't as guilty as he. They'd killed Rossiter and buried him. But they'd done it at his orders.

There wasn't much to choose from between the three. Chuck was their acknowledged leader, but the one Jerome really feared was Curt. Curt's hair, a pale, washed-out yellow, curled around his big, protruding ears. It was almost gray with dirt and looked as though he hadn't bothered to comb it for a week. Curt's eyes were almost the color of his hair. When those eyes were fixed on him, as they usually were, Jerome felt like a mouse being tormented by a cat just before it is eaten.

Al was big, not even looking like a Grego. He was taller than Jerome, and fifteen or twenty pounds heavier. He ran to fat around the middle, but he was the most powerful man Jerome had ever known. He'd thrown a man through the window into the street at the Silver Dollar once about a year ago.

Jerome said, 'He sold his gun this morning. He's unarmed.'

The Grego brothers began to grin.

Jerome said warningly, 'He can get another fast enough. Don't forget it. Don't give him a chance.'

Chuck chuckled. 'We'll take him, gun or no gun. The thing about these gunmen is that they live by a code. Everything has to be a fair fight, and the fastest or most accurate man wins. Only we don't fight that way with gunmen. We'll fight him to win, an' we'll make it look like somethin' personal.'

Jerome's face was relieved. Chuck nodded to Al and Curt, and they shambled out of the office. Chuck sat down on the edge of Jerome's desk and leaned toward him. 'We got our place free and clear out of Rossiter. But this is something else again. One of us might get hurt tangling with Morgan Orr. One of us might get killed.'

Jerome said wearily, 'How much?'

'Oh, I guess a hundred apiece would do it.'

Jerome nodded. 'You'll get it.'

He watched Chuck leave the office. He got up when the door had closed behind him and opened the window. Cool fall air blew into his face, but the unwashed smell of the Grego brothers still clung in his nostrils. He felt unclean—dirty.

Abruptly he turned, got his hat from the tree, and went out the door. He told Jim Brown, the young teller, 'I'm going home. I'll be there if you need me. It's almost time to close, so I doubt if you will.'

Brown nodded, and Jerome went outside. He walked heavily toward home. The feeling was growing in him that he was becoming enmeshed in an ever more complicated set of circumstances designed to conceal his looting of his own bank. First there had been Rossiter. Now it was Morgan Orr. What would it be next?

And yet, he was in too deep to back out now. If word about the bank got out . . . Jerome felt a small chill travel down his spine. The legal penalty for embezzlement was a prison sentence. Only Jerome wouldn't be lucky enough to get off with the legal penalty. Not even if Rossiter's body was never found.

No. A ruined town would exact a more severe penalty from the man who had ruined it. There were times nowadays when Jerome heard that howling mob in his sleep, when he felt the noose tighten around his neck.

He'd wake up when he did, bathed with sweat, clawing at a nonexistent rope around his neck, sometimes babbling incoherent words . . .

Or were they incoherent? He wondered how much Tena had been able to understand—how much she knew.

He came to his gate and went inside. Serena paused in her play on the lawn to stare at him. She didn't run to him any more the way she used to when he came home from work.

He made himself smile, and went to her. He knelt down. 'How's my girl tonight?'

'Fine.' Her eyes, big and unreadable, clung to his face.

He got up, suddenly unable to meet those eyes. God! Why had he been so impatient? He should have stayed out of those shaky mining claim deals over in the mountains. He'd have made it in time, and big too, with just the bank. Now he was an embezzler, a murderer, and soon might be a murderer a second time.

He headed for the porch, but stopped when he saw Dan English approaching along the street. He returned to the gate and waited there.

Dan was plainly angry. Jerome could see that in the way he planted his feet as he walked, in the set of his thick shoulders. Dan reached the gate, stopped and thumbed back his hat. 'Damn you, Mel, you sent for the Gregos, didn't you?'

Jerome looked surprised. 'Me? Why would I send for them?'

'Don't play games with me. I covered up one killin' for you to save the bank and the town, but by God, I won't cover up any more!'

'Dan, what are you talking about?'

The sheriff stared at him contemptuously. 'All three of the Gregos are down at the Buckhorn, shootin' off their mouths about Morgan Orr. As if you didn't know.'

'As a matter of fact, I didn't know, sheriff.'

'I suppose they were in to see you a while ago to pay off their mortgage.' Dan English's voice was loaded with sarcasm.

Jerome said, 'They were. They paid off the last of it today.'

The sheriff snorted. 'All right. Play it that

54

way if you want to. But if anything happens to Morgan Orr, I'll blow this town wide open and you with it. Understand?'

Jerome dropped the pretense suddenly. 'I understand, Dan.'

The sheriff glared at him for a moment, then swung and stalked away. Jerome turned worriedly and went inside.

Tena was waiting for him. There was compassion for him on her face and in her eyes, and for some reason this irritated him. She asked, 'Hard day at the bank?'

He shook his head impatiently. 'No worse than usual.'

She was silent for a moment, another expression in her eyes that angered him more than the compassion had, because this was puzzled fear.

He went over and sat down. He pulled a cigar from his pocket and bit off the end. Still in a pleasant voice, Tena asked, 'What did Dan want?'

He glanced over the match he was holding to the end of the cigar warily. 'Nothing. Why?'

'I just wondered.'

'Well you can stop wondering.'

'All right.' She left the room and went into the kitchen.

He called her back. 'Tena!'

She came back and stood in the doorway, watching him questioningly and uncertainly.

He said, 'You used to know Morgan Orr

didn't you? Before he went away?'

Her face flushed faintly, and then lost color. 'Yes. Why?' Her voice was scarcely more than a whisper.

'Do you think he means it? About settling here, I mean? About changing and giving up his gun?' He stared at her closely, wondering at the obvious agitation in her, and tormented by a sudden stab of jealousy. How well had she known Morgan Orr and what had been between them?

Tena shook her head. 'I don't know, Mel. I don't know whether he means it or not. And even if he does, I don't think the town will let him stay.'

'Do you think they should?' He was probing, now, trying to find justification for that sudden stab of jealousy.

'Yes, I do.' White-faced, tense, she faced him almost defiantly. 'I think any man should have a chance to change if he really wants it.'

'Have you seen him since he came back?'

She hesitated, then nodded.

'Where?'

She hesitated longer this time and at last countered with a question of her own. 'Where do you suppose I saw him?'

'I just asked. No call to get upset, is there?'

'No, I don't suppose there is.' She crossed to him and sat on a footstool at his feet. 'Mel, what's the matter? You've changed in the last six months or so. Is it something I've done?'

He stared at her irritably. He asked nastily, 'Have you done something?'

She flushed darkly, and bit her lip. Then she tried again determinedly. 'Mel, is something wrong at the bank? Is there anything I can do to help?'

His irritability suddenly turned to anger. 'Yes, by God! You can let me alone! You can keep your damn nose out of my business!'

She flinched as though he had struck her. Oddly, it gave him a perverse kind of pleasure to realize he had hurt her. She got up and went into the kitchen.

Confusion built a tension in Jerome's mind. Hell, even if the Gregos did get rid of Morgan Orr what good would it do in the long run? Somebody wanted to know what had become of Rossiter. They wouldn't stop snooping until they found out.

And even if they did stop, it wouldn't solve Jerome's problem. There were the three Grego brothers, sly, greedy. They'd hold Rossiter's killing, and Morgan's, over his head. He'd have to pay and pay to keep them still.

No. He couldn't do that. He wouldn't do it. He wouldn't spend his life working to keep the Gregos in money.

A new idea occurred to him. He could finish looting his bank and go away. He could do that.

Thinking of it, he felt a little better. Still, it wasn't what he wanted. He liked Arapaho

Wells. He was getting to be a big man here. It was a growing country, and he could grow with it.

But he mustn't let things get out of hand. Because if the town ever found out what he had done...

He shuddered, and involuntarily loosened the tight stiff collar which had begun to feel as rough as a hangman's noose.

CHAPTER SIX

The Buckhorn was crowded, though it was only a little after five. A piano tinkled in the L-shaped part of the room beside the bar, played by an attractive woman in a low-cut gown. A cowboy hung over the piano, singing the song she was playing in a reedy, but not unpleasant voice.

Morgan stepped quickly to the bar. The feeling of apprehension was stronger in him now. He knew he was a fool for stepping into the Gregos' trap. But he knew, too, that sooner or later he had to face and take whatever the town proposed to give him.

Len Smith brought him a beer instead of sliding it down the bar. Len's round face was scared and sweating. He said, 'Morg, drink it fast and git. They're laying for you. They know you sold your gun.'

Morgan nodded. 'Thanks, Len.' Smith was the second to offer a friendly word of advice. It helped just to know the town wasn't a hundred per cent against him.

He sipped his beer, looking around carefully. Curt Grego was down at the end of the bar, facing him. Curt's hungry eyes clung to his face insolently, hopefully.

Chuck was at the other end of the bar. Holding his glass, Morgan swung around, and saw Al, the big one, sitting at a table near the door.

However he turned, he'd have his back to at least one of them. And he understood that this was the way they wanted it.

He waited. Talk went on around him, but it was guarded talk—and forced. All eyes watched him surreptitiously, and with veiled dislike.

He saw Roy Forette down next to Chuck Grego. Forette had a half smile on his wide mouth, as though this pleased him. this feeling of unrelieved tension. Morgan could still see the appraisal in his eyes, and its meaning was unmistakable.

Chuck Grego's voice raised suddenly, 'Hey Morg!'

Morgan looked at him, knowing this was it. He felt the muscles in his arms go tense. He reminded himself deliberately that no gun hung at his side today.

As though at a signal, the saloon was deathly

still. The piano player's hands rested motionless, tense upon the keys. The singing cowboy's face had turned a little white.

Chuck no longer had to shout. He said, 'We been havin' a little argument, Morg. Mebbe you can help us.'

Morgan glanced at Roy Forette. Roy's eyes were very bright. He licked his lips, slowly and carefully.

Morgan said, 'All right.'

Grego said, 'We been wondering about guts, and whether losin' 'em is what makes a gunman give up his gun.'

Morgan's face hardened. He said softly, 'Never mind going through all the motions, Chuck. You want a fight. I'll accommodate you.'

Chuck said, 'Slide 'im your gun, Roy.'

Morgan stepped away from the bar. 'Nope. Not that way.' He smiled inwardly, with rueful cynicism, knowing that Chuck's bullet would have smashed into his chest before he ever touched the sliding gun.

And he appraised the situation swiftly in his mind. He disliked the idea of starting the fight himself, because it would give credibility to the things the townspeople were already saying about him. But he knew, as well, that if he did not take the initiative, they'd beat him to death, or toss him a gun and catch him in their crossfire before he could use it.

His mouth twisted. Damned if he did,

60

damned if he didn't. Still, a bad reputation was better than being dead.

With no hesitation whatever, he sprang into action. He drove across the floor, directly at Chuck.

Behind him, Curt Grego shouted, a wordless cry of balked fury. But Morgan was moving fast, and paid no heed.

He struck Chuck with the point of his shoulder just as Chuck's gun cleared its holster. He drove Chuck back against the bar with a crash that shook the ponderous thing and spilled liquor from glasses all along the length of it.

Chuck's gun, out of its holster, came up in a wild, unthinking arc, and smashed against Morgan's forehead.

It stunned him and drove him back. He recovered quickly, as an animal does, and slashed with an elbow at Chuck's throat, continuing the motion of his arm afterward until his hand locked on Chuck's right wrist.

Yanking now, ignoring the gun still clutched in Chuck's hand, he pivoted, turning Chuck with the violence of his swing. He seized the upper part of Chuck's arm with his left hand, raising his knee as he did.

Savagely then, with brutal efficiency, he brought Chuck's arm down against his rising knee.

A scream tore from Chuck's drooling mouth, its sound mingling with the audible

61

crack of his forearm breaking. The gun clattered to the floor.

Morgan pushed Chuck from him violently and swung around, fully aware that this had just begun. Al Grego was coming, indeed had almost reached him. Down at the far end of the bar, Curt was trying to get a shot at him through the milling crowd.

Morgan sidestepped that first, bull-like rush of Al Grego. As he did, he raised both hands, clasped together. He slammed them down on the top of Al's head with all the force of which he was capable.

Al's head, already low, was driven nearly a foot lower by the force of the blow—low enough to crash head-on into the walnut bar.

The force of his own momentum nearly knocked him senseless. He crumpled down the bar and sat on the rail before it, shaking his great shaggy head with stupid confusion. He looked up at Morgan, glared, then started up.

Morgan raised a knee. It caught Al squarely in the face, lifting him nearly six inches. Al's nose burst like a tomato, and again his head banged against the bar.

Down the bar, a shot blasted. Morgan felt a sharp, burning sensation along his thigh, and immediately afterward the warm wetness of blood.

And the crowd, caught up by the wildness of the moment, like wolves with the smell of blood in their nostrils, closed around him.

Panting, Morgan backed against the bar. He was shocked by the things he saw in the eyes of those before him.

He had lived by the gun—had made his life one of violence and death. All the while, he had envied people like these men before him—envied them their peaceful way of life.

Never had he suspected the latent savagery in each of them. He had not conceived how quickly their peaceful exterior could be stripped away to reveal the violence beneath.

Again Morgan brought the fight to them, though he knew he couldn't win. Thrusting against the bar behind him, he drove himself out into the midst of them, striking with fists and elbows, kicking, kneeing.

Their voices rose in an eerie kind of cry that had no separate words, and this was the sound of a blood-mad mob. This was the sound that Mel Jerome often heard in his sleep.

They came from all sides, and surrounded Morgan Orr, each strangely eager, each seeming to need the stimulus of striking him, of beating him down to the floor. He sank to his knees.

A sound like thunder stopped the kicks and blows, and slowly the men standing above him moved away.

Dan English stood in the door, a double-barreled shotgun in his hands. Smoke curled from one muzzle. Plaster dust trickled down from the ceiling over Morgan's head.

English spoke to the bartender. 'Len, get a door and someone to help you. Carry him over to the hotel.'

There was a time of silence for Morgan. Then he felt himself being helped to his feet and half-carried out into the cool, evening air. The sun was down, but a touch of pink still lingered on a few high clouds. He thought thickly that he must have been in the Buckhorn less than twenty minutes.

And then, mercifully, unconsciousness took him.

*   *   *

Dan English surveyed the crowd angrily, the shotgun cradled in his arms. Over by the bar, Chuck Grego was getting to his feet, his face twisted with pain from his broken arm. Al Grego, blood streaming from a broken nose, was on hands and knees, shaking his ponderous head. Curt, his face a study of balked fury, stood spread-legged, shifting his wicked glance from the sheriff to the door and back again.

The rest of the crowd, some of them nursing minor hurts inflicted by Morgan Orr's fists and knees, were sheepishly dispersing. Dan English roared, 'Wait a minute, God damn you! Don't go sneaking out of here until I've had my say!'

They swung to face him. Some of them were sullen, some ashamed, some defiant.

64

Dan said, 'The Gregos, I can understand. A meaner bunch of bastards never lived. But I'd like to hear the excuses the rest of you have got.'

A man grumbled, 'Morgan started it.'

'Like hell he did! Morgan's had enough killing, enough fighting. Don't tell me Morgan started it!'

He looked at them disgustedly, revulsion in his eyes. He had seen a mob as he walked in the door, a murderous, unthinking mob with only one thought in its collective head—to destroy Morgan Orr—to beat him, hurt him, kill him.

Why? English shook his head. A mob didn't need a reason. All they needed was someone to whip them up into a frenzy. The Gregos had taken care of that.

The sheriff bit his lip, fighting back his fury. No use to scold them. They were ashamed enough already. No use to jail them. Hell, you couldn't jail half the men in a town. No use to talk reason to them. Mobs have no reason.

English said harshly, 'Curt, get over there and help Al to his feet. Then the three of you get down to the jail.'

'What's the charge, Sheriff?' Curt's voice was insolent, and he put sarcastic emphasis on the word, 'sheriff.'

Dan swung the shotgun. 'Shut your ugly mouth! I'll think of a charge. In the meantime keep still or you'll never reach the jail.' His eyes left no doubt that he meant it.

Curt went over and helped Al to his feet. He steered him toward the door. Chuck, carefully holding his broken right arm steady with his left hand, followed, his face gray.

Dan English broke the shotgun and inserted a fresh shell in place of the one he had fired. Then, closing it with a snap, he followed them up the street.

The crowd that had gathered before the Buckhorn parted to let them through. Dan spoke to a man as he passed him, 'Ira, go over to the hotel and tell Doc I've got some work for him down at the jail when he gets through with Morgan Orr.'

'Sure, Dan.' The man headed for the hotel.

Dan walked behind the Grego brothers down Second to the jail. He opened the door and watched them walk inside. Standing just inside the door, the shotgun ready, he said, 'Leave your guns and belts on the table there.'

Curt and Al unbuckled theirs and tossed them on the table. Then Curt went over and helped Chuck with his. English said, 'Back into the jail. Move, damn you!'

He herded them all into one of the two cells and banged the door shut behind them.

Chuck looked at him, hatred strong in his pain-filled eyes. He said softly, 'You let us out of here, Dan. You let us out. All we got to do is spill...'

Dan English swung the shotgun. 'Spill what, you son of a bitch?'

Chuck looked at the gaping muzzles, then up to the sheriff's eyes, now like bullets looking out of a revolver cylinder. He grumbled something and sat down on the bench.

Dan English said softly, 'Just remember this when you start to spill your guts. Remember that mob in the saloon tonight. How would it be if you spilled what you know about the bank? How would it be if they knew you an' Mel Jerome were hand in glove? You think they gave Morgan Orr a bad time? Think what they'd do to you.'

He waited, but none of the Gregos spoke.

He laughed bitterly. 'So go ahead. Talk whenever you've a mind to.'

He went back into his office, lighted a lamp and carried it back into the jail. He set it up on a shelf built especially for that purpose.

He returned and sat down, feeling his anger drain out of him, feeling the beginning of self revulsion over the violent passions that had claimed him so completely in the last half hour. That was what came of keeping a secret such as that of Mel Jerome and the Grego brothers. It was what came of going against your conscience, against all of the principles upon which you have built your life.

He heard a step on the walk outside and looking up, saw Lily Leslie, who played the piano at the Buckhorn, standing at the door.

She came in. 'Dan, what gets into people? The Buckhorn is a shambles.'

He got up with instinctive courtesy, and the vagrant thought crossed his mind that it would be good to have a woman like this to come home to, to share your troubles with. It wasn't the first time such a thought had come into his head. But he always put it uneasily away. Lily was a piano player in a saloon. So far as he knew, that was as far as it went. But Dan always caught himself wondering about her past, the things she had done, the men she had known.

He said, 'You tell me, Lily. I don't know. I guess it's fear that pushes them into things like what happened tonight. They're afraid of Morgan Orr. They're afraid of what his staying will mean to the town.'

'Chuck Grego claims he's lying about why he wants to stay. He suggested that Morgan's just here to look things over for a gang of outlaws.'

Dan English laughed mockingly. 'Sure. That's likely. So he sells his gun and lets himself get beat up because of it!'

'What do you think, Dan?'

Dan frowned. 'I think he's telling the truth. I think he wants to forget he ever wore a gun.'

'Will he make it stick?'

Dan shook his head. 'I don't see how he can. Not with the town feeling the way it does about him. Roy Forette keeps watching him and I know what Roy's thinking—that if he killed Morgan Orr he'd have it made. He'd be top gun.' He sighed. 'Then there's the Grego brothers. They'll never give up now until Morgan's dead.'

She smiled softly. 'Poor Dan. And you're in the middle.'

He nodded, a little embarrassed but grateful for her understanding.

She turned toward the door, a tall, slender woman whose chief beauty was the softness of her face and eyes, the gentleness of her mouth. 'I've got to get back. I just wanted to be sure you were all right.'

'I'm all right.' He looked at her, wanting her to stay, but not knowing how to hold her. He said, 'I wish...'

'What, Dan?'

He flushed slightly. 'Nothing. I'll see you later, Lily.'

'Yes.' She went outside and walked toward Main.

Dan sat scowling in his swivel chair. He suddenly hated Jerome and the Gregos with virulent intensity. But he hated himself even more.

He knew now what he should have done. When he found out about Rossiter, he should have jailed Jerome and the Gregos and charged them with murder. He should have let the bank fail.

Then he remembered the way that mob had looked in the Buckhorn Saloon less than half an hour before. A small chill ran along his spine. God help Jerome, the Gregos, and yes, even himself, if they ever found out about the bank.

CHAPTER SEVEN

When Morgan Orr came to, he was in his room at the hotel. He laid still for a few moments, dazed and feeling pain in almost every part of his body. A lamp burned on the dresser but there was no one in the room.

There was a heavy bandage on his left thigh—the bullet wound, he supposed.

He threw back the covers and looked at himself. He saw the mean-looking bruises, some abrasions, and he silently thanked Dan English for saving him from worse.

He grinned wryly. Hearing the door, he hastily pulled the covers up.

A woman came in, and it was a moment before he recognized the piano player at the Buckhorn. She glanced at him and smiled pleasantly. 'The Buckhorn's a wreck. They won't be needing me for a day or two, so if you like I'll take care of you.'

Morgan said, 'I can't ...'

'Pay me? Did I say anything about that?'

'No, but ...'

'Be quiet now. You took a bad beating. You need to rest.'

'I got off lightly, considering.'

'Yes,' she said quietly.

'What time is it?' Morgan asked.

'About nine. Why?'

He grimaced. 'I've only been in Arapaho Wells about twelve hours. An awful lot has happened.'

She got his Bull Durham out of his torn, crumpled shirt on the floor and expertly rolled a cigarette. She twisted the ends, stuck it between his lips and held a match to it.

He dragged the smoke deep into his lungs gratefully. He squinted at her through a cloud of smoke. 'Why?'

She didn't pretend to misunderstand. 'Why am I taking care of you?' She shrugged, then smiled. 'We're two of a kind, you and I. We bear a label. Maybe I'm interested in seeing whether or not you succeed in getting the label off. Because if you do, I might have a chance to do the same.'

He felt a strange kinship with her. She took the cigarette out of his mouth and tossed it into the porcelain pot beneath the bed without self-consciousness.

She said, 'There's another reason too, I guess. I didn't like the looks I saw on all those faces in the saloon tonight.' Her face was sober now, a little frightened. She put up a slender hand and smoothed her glossy reddish hair.

Morgan said, 'It won't make you any more popular with the town to be taking care of me.'

71

Anger touched her face. 'Do you think I care?'

Morgan smiled. 'The label. You don't want it stuck any tighter, do you?'

'To hell with the label! If I have to go against what I think is right to get it off, it's going to have to stay.'

Drowsiness touched Morgan. His eyelids drooped, and he blinked. The woman said, 'I'll get out and let you sleep. But I'll look in every hour or so in case you want anything. Don't get out of bed. You'll only hurt yourself more.'

He grinned. 'Thanks ... uh ... What is your name, by the way?'

'Lily. Lily Leslie.'

'Your real name.'

She flushed ever so slightly. 'Maggie.'

He said, 'All right, Maggie.' His eyes were determined. 'I'll get the label off, and you will too.'

She blew out the lamp and went out. He heard her steps along the hall diminishing. He heard a door close.

He stared up at the ceiling. He thought of the Gregos, and anger touched him, making his blood beat faster. Then he thought of Lily Leslie, and of Dan English, and of Si Booth. Of Len Smith, the bartender in the Buckhorn. Nothing was all bad, or all good either, for that matter. People were people, reacting to a lot of different things. Like fear. Fear had been behind the actions of most of the men in the

72

Buckhorn tonight. Fear of Morgan Orr. Fear of what his staying would mean to their peaceful town.

But the Gregos—they were different. There was something behind their planned and obvious baiting of him tonight. Someone wanted him out of town for a specific and altogether personal reason.

Jerome. Was it possible Jerome knew the truth—knew that Serena was Morgan Orr's daughter?

He heard heavy steps on the stairs. They came along the hall and stopped at the door of his room.

For an instant, panic touched him. He was in no condition to defend himself. He would not be able to move fast enough to escape death if that someone outside the door wanted to kill him.

He had no gun. And the door was unlocked.

He braced himself and waited.

The door opened stealthily, squeaking slightly on its hinges. Morgan strained his eyes to see whoever was there, but all he could make out was a blurred and shapeless form. He tensed himself, intending to fling himself off the bed at the stranger's first hostile move.

The man came in, closing the door softly behind him.

Morgan was suddenly furious. Helpless, unable to defend himself, still he could have his anger, and could say his say. He asked harshly,

73

'What the hell do *you* want?'

The man started—whirled. He said, 'I didn't know whether you were awake or not. Sorry.' It was Dan English's voice.

Dan stepped to the dresser and struck a match. He lighted the lamp and trimmed the wick. Then he turned.

He pulled out the straight-backed chair beside the small table and straddled it. He grinned at Morgan ever so faintly. 'You look like bloody hell!'

'I feel like it too.' A residue of anger lingered in Morgan and made him say, 'You ought to know better than to come sneaking into a man's room in the middle of the night. If I'd had a gun I'd probably have killed you.'

'I knew you didn't have a gun.'

Morgan's anger did not subside. 'What do you want?'

The sheriff looked at him helplessly. 'Damned if I know, Morg. Maybe I just wanted to see how bad you were. I've got the Grego brothers over in jail. Chuck's arm is broken, and so is Al's nose.'

Morgan said, 'Aren't you going to ask about the fight?'

'I know what it was about.'

'Well, if you know that, you know a damn sight more than I do. What was it about?'

English shrugged. 'Can't tell you, Morg. But I can tell you one thing. You better get out of town as soon as you can walk. Chuck Grego won't forget his broken arm any more than Al will forget his nose or the way you kicked him around. Curt's got no more scruples than a diamond-back. You're a dead man if you stay.'

Morgan's jaw hardened. 'You came up here to tell me that? What kind of a goddam sheriff are you, anyway, to stand there and admit to me you can't keep me alive if I decide to stay in your town?'

Dan English flinched, but his eyes met Morgan's without wavering. 'A bad sheriff maybe. But a realistic one. A company of cavalry couldn't keep you alive if you decide to stay. I know. Hell, you can find another town. A better town than this.' There was a tone of pleading in the sheriff's voice.

But Morgan shook his head. 'They're all alike. And this is the one I want.'

'I can't keep the Gregos longer than tomorrow morning. All I can charge them with is disturbing the peace—that is unless you want to sign an assault complaint.'

Morgan grinned. 'They didn't assault me. I never gave them a chance. I assaulted them.'

The sheriff didn't return his grin. 'All right, Morg. Treat it lightly if you want. But don't say I didn't warn you.' He got up and pushed the chair back against the table.

At the door, he turned with his hand on the knob. 'Think it over, Morg. Do that much for me. Think it over and let me know tomorrow.'

Morgan nodded, but he knew he'd never

change. He was going to stay, even if it killed him.

CHAPTER EIGHT

Chuck Grego didn't sleep at all that night. He sat on the edge of his cot in the jail cell and listened to his brothers' snores with mounting fury.

His arm pained steadily. The doc had set it, splinted it, and put it in a sling, but he'd given him nothing for the pain. Chuck had tried to sleep for a while, but had failed because of the pain. At last he'd given up and spent the hours staring into the darkness and nursing his hates. Hate for Morgan, for the sheriff and for Mel Jerome. Hate for his brothers for not winning the fight.

His fury reached new heights when Dan English came in the morning, released them roughly, and returned their guns.

The sheriff followed them to the door and stood, watching them. Then called, 'Get out of town.'

Chuck turned, defiant now that the three of them were armed again. He said, 'You go to hell.'

Dan stepped out onto the walk. 'Want to try me, Chuck?' His eyes were bits of stone.

Chuck growled, 'No. But by God nobody's going to tell me to get out of town.'

76

'I'm telling you.'

Chuck turned his back. English said, 'Nine o'clock. That's the deadline.'

Chuck went on up the street, muttering savagely to himself, his voice laden with sarcasm. 'That's the deadline! In a pig's butt! Deadline! Who the hell does he think he is?'

Curt's voice was soft. 'You're not thinkin' very straight, Chuck. You want to take on both the sheriff and Morgan Orr with a broken arm?'

'Broken arm be damned. There's nothin' wrong with you.'

'Huh uh. And there ain't going to be, either. Don't think I'm going to take either of them on by myself. Not in a fight.'

'Who said anything about a fight?'

Curt shook his shaggy head. 'It'd be better to go home and think about it for a day or two. Figure something out.'

Chuck turned and stared at him scathingly. 'I don't suppose you'd mind seeing Jerome, would you? I don't suppose you'd mind having that hundred?'

'No, I wouldn't mind that.' Curt was unruffled.

'Then come on.'

Furiously Chuck led the way up to Main, along it to Third and thence along Third to Jerome's big house. Though it was not yet seven o'clock, he banged on the door heavily with his left fist. When that failed to bring an immediate answer, he began to kick it with his boot.

He heard a protesting voice behind it, and it opened slightly. Jerome's young wife said, 'What is it? What do you want?'

'We want to see Jerome. Get him down here.'

The door closed. Chuck paced the porch angrily. At last Jerome appeared, clad in a bathrobe. 'What is this? What's the big idea of coming here...'

'Save it!' Chuck said harshly. He pushed into the house. 'We want to talk to you. Now.'

Jerome's hair was tousled from sleeping, his face showing a stubble of whiskers. His eyes were briefly angry, but did not stay that way for very long. He said hastily, 'All right, all right. Come on in here.'

He led the way into a room off the parlor and closed the door. Apparently it was a combination office and study. There was a desk against one wall, and behind it, several shelves of books.

Jerome stood with his back against the door. He looked at Chuck. 'You fool! You bungle a fight with Morgan Orr and the minute you're out of jail you come running to me. Don't you realize how that's going to look?'

'To hell with how it looks. We want our money—and something extra for my broken arm and Al's busted nose.'

Jerome's eyes sparkled. 'You'll get nothing.

78

Morgan Orr is still alive.'

Chuck advanced on him threateningly. Jerome stood fast. His face was white, but his mouth was set determinedly. Had Chuck been more observing, he would have realized that Jerome had been pushed too far. Jerome was in a corner, and knew it, and now would fight. He said, 'Talk if you want to. Go on downtown and spill your guts. Tell everybody you killed Rossiter and that I told you to. Tell them the bank is broke and they've all lost their money. You think you'd get out of town?' He laughed bitterly. 'They'd tear you to pieces. Maybe they would come after me, but they'd get you first.'

Chuck said, 'Maybe not. Maybe they'd come after you first.' He didn't really believe that, and he could see in Jerome's face that the banker knew he didn't.

Jerome pressed his advantage. 'Now get out of here and don't come back. I'm not afraid of you any more. I'm not afraid at all. You'll get your hundred apiece if and when you finish what you started last night on Morgan Orr. But not until you do.'

Chuck said, 'Maybe he'll leave. He's sure beat up.'

Jerome just looked at him for a long time then slowly opened the door and stood aside.

Chuck went out, knowing he was beaten, temporarily at least. But he'd think of a way. There had to be some way to get even with Morgan Orr, the sheriff, and Mel Jerome too.

He walked downtown, his brothers at his heels. He hunkered down on the walk in front of the Buckhorn, tipped his hat against the brightness of the sun in the street and waited. It was seven-thirty now. The Buckhorn would open at eight. He had an hour and a half before the sheriff's deadline at nine.

*   *   *

Tena Jerome was terrified when the noise awoke her, but she was even more terrified when she saw the three villainous looking Grego brothers on the porch.

She was startled when her husband let them in, and took them into his study.

She started back upstairs and then, remembering the look of fear that had been in her husband's eyes, got his shotgun from the closet and loaded it with trembling hands. She crept to the study door and put her ear to the panels. She didn't know what she would do if trouble developed, but she did know she'd do something. There were two shells in the shotgun, and she'd use them both if she needed to.

She heard voices behind the panel, first her husband's, then the voice that had demanded on the porch that she call Jerome. As she listened, her hands grew cold and trembled against the gun.

She had been right in her doubts the other

80

day. The bank was ruined. Rossiter, the bank examiner, had been murdered at her husband's orders. And Morgan Orr had been badly beaten and even now might be dead.

Hastily she backed away from the door. Quietly she returned the gun to the closet, having presence of mind enough to unload it first.

Then, in bare feet and wrapper, she ran upstairs. She snatched up her clothes, her shoes and a comb, and ran back down.

She could hear them leaving. She slipped quickly into the kitchen and began to dress. Jerome's heavy steps sounded on the stairs.

When she had finished, Tena ran a comb quickly through her hair and pinned it swiftly into a bun at her neck. Then she went out the back door. She had to know about Morgan— had to know if he was all right. She had to tell someone what was happening.

She prayed silently as she hurried along the street—that Morgan was all right—that he wouldn't die. She prayed for guidance, so that she would know if she was doing right. She hated to betray her husband, but he was playing too dangerous a game, as Tena well knew. The Grego brothers were deadly and unscrupulous. If they had killed Rossiter, they certainly wouldn't hesitate to kill Jerome.

Morgan would know what to do. Men like the Gregos were not unfamiliar to a man who had lived as Morgan Orr had lived. And she couldn't go to the sheriff, for that would mean prison for her husband, or death by hanging.

Distraught and close to tears, Tena went into the back door of the hotel. She prayed she wouldn't see anyone, but she had to take that chance. She went up the back stairs and halted at the top.

There was no one in the hall, so she tiptoed along it and opened Morgan's door.

He lay sleeping on the bed, the covers thrown back so that his upper body was visible. His face, though beaten and bruised, was relaxed. All the hardness apparent in it when he was awake was gone.

Tena watched him for a moment, the door at her back. A wave of tenderness washed over her, and pity for Morgan. He had troubles enough of his own, and now she was bringing him more.

But there was no one else to whom she could turn. There was no one but Morgan.

Standing there by the door she said softly and timidly, 'Morgan. Morgan, it's me.'

He stirred and opened his eyes.

For an instant after he awakened, Morgan stared at her in disbelief. Then he turned, raised on an elbow, his face twisting with pain. He said, 'Tena! My God, are you crazy? You shouldn't be here!'

He saw the terror, the awful confusion in her eyes, then, and his face hardened. 'What is it? What's happened?'

82

She appeared to be holding onto herself with desperation that almost amounted to panic. He had the feeling she was close to running across the room and flinging herself into his arms.

His clothes, which Lily Leslie had apparently washed and ironed during the night, lay folded on the chair. Morgan said, his voice carefully neutral and without emotion. 'Hand me my clothes and get hold of yourself.'

'You shouldn't get up. You might hurt...'

'I feel better this morning.' And he did. There was still pain, his muscles were stiff and sore, but his head was clear.

She picked up the clothes and brought them to him, flushing slightly and not meeting his eyes. Then she went to the window and stared unhappily down into the street.

Morgan threw the covers back and began to dress. There was an intimacy about this of which both were acutely aware.

And there was anger growing in Morgan Orr—anger at whoever had frightened Tena.

He finished dressing and sat on the edge of the bed to pull on his boots. He was a little surprised at the recovery he had made. He wasn't ready to take on the town again just yet, but neither was he going to stay in bed all day.

He said, 'Tell me about it.'

She turned from the window. She was crying now, softly and silently. 'My husband hired the Gregos to kill you.'

Morgan's eyes widened slightly. 'Why? Does he know ...?'

'About us? No, Morgan. He doesn't know that.' She paced back and forth across the room.

He said gently, 'What is it, then? Tell me. Maybe I can help.' He wanted desperately to take her in his arms and comfort her, but he didn't move.

'Mel's bank is broke. Ruined. About six months ago, a bank examiner named Rossiter came here to check his accounts. He spent a day in the bank and that night he disappeared.'

Morgan made a long, low whistle.

Tena went on determinedly. 'I found out this morning that Mel had hired the Grego brothers to kill him. They did, but nothing happened. No one came to check up on Rossiter's disappearance. No one even seemed to miss him. So when Mel heard you had come to town—well, he just jumped to the conclusion that you'd been sent to find out what happened to Rossiter.'

'And that's why he tried to have me killed?' Morgan's voice was filled with amazement.

'That's why. Now the Grego brothers are threatening Mel. And I don't know what to do. Oh God, I don't know what to do!'

Morgan frowned. There wasn't anything she *could* do. Her husband, and the Gregos, were guilty of murder. Jerome was also guilty of ... or was he? Morgan asked, 'The bank—how did

84

it get into trouble?'

Tena shook her head. 'I don't know for sure. I thought it was making money. Mel always said it was. Then he began taking trips over to the mining camps in the mountains...'

Morgan said, 'Speculating in mining claims, probably. And he lost, not only his own money, but the bank's too.'

He was remembering the crowd in the Buckhorn last night, remembering the looks on their faces, the hysteria that had gripped them. He was realizing that they'd react even more violently than that if they knew they had been ruined by Jerome, if they knew the bank was completely broke.

He opened his mouth to speak, but the words he intended to say were never uttered. A soft knock sounded on the door.

He got to his feet so suddenly that pain from the flesh wound in his thigh shot clear through his body. He seized Tena's arm and pulled her over beside the door. Then he opened it.

Dan English stood in the hall. It only took one look at his face to tell Morgan he had been standing there listening—long enough to know everything that had been said in this room.

He said, 'You better come in, Dan, and hear it all. You'd better come in. Your town is like a keg of powder and somebody's about to light the fuse.'

CHAPTER NINE

Dan English came in. His face was gray, and his hands, as he rolled himself a smoke, were trembling.

Looking at him, suspicion was born in Morgan Orr. He said, 'You knew about Rossiter, didn't you? How much did you get paid?' He was getting angry now, angry at Dan English who had sold himself out.

Dan's face flushed. His eyes turned hot. 'Damn you, Morg, you can't...'

'Why can't I?'

'Because it isn't true. I didn't sell out.'

'But you knew.' Morgan's voice was cold.

Tena was watching this, white-faced, shaken. Dan English looked at her, then back at Morgan. 'Yes. I knew. But not at the time it was done. I figured something had happened to Rossiter and started an investigation. Jerome got all mixed up in his stories and finally broke down and spilled the whole thing.'

Tena broke in, 'But why didn't you do something? Why didn't you arrest him, and the Grego brothers?'

For a few moments Dan English didn't reply. At last he said, 'What good would it have done, aside from making them pay for the killing? Ever see a run on a bank, Mrs Jerome? Ever see a country ruined because a bank goes bust? I have, and there'd been no stealing in that bank, either. All it took was a little rumor that the bank was shaky. First thing you know, everybody in the country wanted their money. The bank couldn't pay it. So they went broke.' He looked at Morgan, his eyes getting defiant. 'I didn't want to see that happen here. I figured if Jerome had time, maybe some of those bad investments he made with the bank's funds would pay off. It was worth the chance. Jerome could be jailed anytime. So could the Grego brothers.'

Shaken, Morgan said, 'But you'd have to have done something eventually. Somebody must have missed Rossiter. Even if they didn't—even if they figured he'd disappeared voluntarily—run off with a woman or something, they were sure to send another bank examiner at some time.'

Dan nodded. 'You think it's been easy? Every time a stranger comes to town, I wonder if he's the one. And when that mob last night, working on you...' He pulled out a bandanna and mopped his forehead. 'If they can be worked up that easy, what are they going to do when they find out Jerome has ruined them?'

Morgan looked at Tena. 'You'd better go home before you're missed. No use in you getting mixed up in this.'

She tried to smile and failed. 'I'm mixed up in it already. Morgan, what are we going to do?'

87

He shook his head. 'I don't know. But I'm glad you came.' He put into his glance all the things he couldn't put into words. Dan English watched closely.

Morgan didn't know how much the sheriff had figured out, and discovered he didn't care. He was glad he had come back, because Tena needed his help. If violence erupted in Arapaho Wells, it could touch Tena and her daughter. A mob is never kind, and Tena was Jerome's wife.

She went to the door and opened it. Morgan crossed the room quickly and looked out into the hall. He turned. 'All clear. Go on now. Hurry.'

He took her face between his hands and kissed her lightly on the forehead. With the tips of his fingers, he wiped the tears from her cheeks. 'Go on.'

She hurried down the hall toward the back stairs. Morgan closed the door and faced the sheriff. Dan said, 'So that's the way it is.'

Morgan's eyes turned hard. He said evenly, 'I knew Tena before she ever met Jerome.'

Dan accepted the implied warning. He asked, changing the subject abruptly, 'What are you going to do, Morg? You've got no reason to love this town and now you've got it in your power to ruin it and everyone in it.'

'You think that would make me feel better?'

'Depends.'

'On what?'

'On how bitter you are. On what kind of man

you really are. On how bad you want Jerome's wife...'

Morgan tensed, and the sheriff said quickly, 'No sir. You couldn't win, Morg. Not in the shape you're in. Besides I've got a gun.'

Morgan muttered furiously. 'Then watch your tongue!'

'Don't you want her, Morg?' The sheriff's eyes told Morgan he was fully aware that he was on shaky ground. Further, that he didn't care. This was too important to him to mince words about it.

Morgan answered truthfully. 'I want her more than anything else in the world.'

'And if Jerome was dead, you could have her.' Dan English was watching Morgan closely. Morgan felt as though his very soul was being probed.

It angered him. He said furiously, 'I don't want her over the body of her husband. I don't want her over a ruined town. What kind of a goddam man do you think I am? Just because I've lived by my gun, do you think I'd do anything?'

'Most gunmen would.'

'Well, this one wouldn't. Now what the hell do you want? I won't leave town, if that's what you've got in mind.'

'Just keep still, Morg. Just keep still.'

'All right! I'll keep still. But you'd better figure out something better than that, Dan. Because it won't do. The secret isn't going to be a secret forever.'

Dan English wasn't elated. He was a beaten man. He said wearily, 'You think I don't know that?'

'And when the town finds out, they're going to blame you just as much as they blame Jerome.'

'I know that too.' Dan English walked wearily to the door and put his hand on the knob. He made a thin smile. 'I hope you make it, Morg. I really hope you do.'

Morgan nodded. 'Thanks. I'll wish the same for you.'

The sheriff went out, closing the door behind him. Morgan went to the window and stared moodily down into the street.

He knew it was his own imagination, but there seemed to be a certain feel in the air this morning that had not been there yesterday morning when he walked down Main carrying his saddle.

And the old sixth sense was working at him—the animal warning that there was trouble in the air, and danger. A peaceful Sunday—or so it looked. But Morgan knew it would not be peaceful. By night, he doubted if anyone would even know it was Sunday.

At the upper end of Main, the church bell began to toll, and it was a comforting sound that seemed to drive the menace from the town. Morgan supposed they rang it an hour before church began, for it was now just eight o'clock.

He looked down the street. There were several men in front of the Buckhorn, which was opening its doors. He couldn't fail to recognize them—the three Grego brothers and his father, Sam Orr. They filed inside the Buckhorn and again the street was deserted.

He was acutely aware of one thing. Too many people shared the secret of Rossiter's murder and the condition of the bank for it to remain a secret long. The Grego brothers were threatening Jerome. Jerome himself might be getting panicky. And Tena was plainly scared.

He turned and limped to the door. His body was still sore and he couldn't move easily without experiencing pain somewhere. But it was pain he could stand.

He went slowly down the stairs. The lobby was deserted. He went out into the sunlight and stood on the veranda while he rolled and lighted a smoke. Then he stepped down on the walk and headed for the restaurant. None of yesterday's problems were solved—he still needed a job badly—he still felt keenly the hostility of everyone he passed on the street. They stared at him with empty faces and empty eyes in a way that was almost animal.

Si Booth was at the restaurant counter, working on a stack of buckwheat cakes and a big patty of sausage. He glanced up as Morgan came in, then indicated the stool beside him. 'You look better than I thought you would. I was comin' over to the hotel as soon as I'd et.'

Morgan sat down. The woman who ran the restaurant apparently knew who he was today, for there was a changed quality in the way she looked at him, and again he sensed hostility.

He guessed he couldn't blame her much—or anyone else for that matter. He was trouble for their town. He'd already proved that.

Si said, 'So now what? Still going to stay?'

Morgan nodded. He picked up his coffee cup and sipped.

Si said, 'Next time...'

Morgan nodded. 'Next time Dan might not be around to interfere. I know that. It's a chance I'll have to take. But they'll get used to me. They'll have to.'

Si shrugged, unconvinced. 'If they don't kill you first.'

Morgan didn't reply.

Si was silent a long time. At last he said, 'Reckon I'm a damn fool for sayin' this. But I keep rememberin' the way it started—right down there in the stable ten years ago. You didn't ask for that fight. You didn't have no choice.'

Morgan asked, 'A fool for saying what, Si?'

'Why, this. If things get too damn tough— well, I got twenty or thirty broncs out at Spear. Jess has been pasturin' 'em for me. They got to be broke sometime an' this fall is as good a time as any. You say the word an' we'll run 'em in. You break 'em down in my corral, an' gentle 'em. I'll pay five dollars a head.'

'The town won't like it, Si.'

'To hell with the town!' Si mopped his plate with the last forkful of buckwheat cake and stuffed it in his mouth.

A kind of pleasant warmth spread through Morgan Orr. He wasn't used to saying thanks, but it wasn't hard right now. He said, 'That's decent, Si. I'll break them right. You can count on it.'

Si grunted sourly. He got up, paid for his meal and left without another word.

Morgan stared at his plate, puzzled at the way decency and savagery conflicted in human beings. Up to now he'd seen a lot of the greed and cruelty—not very much of the decency.

But maybe that was partly his own fault. Maybe he hadn't looked for it. In spite of that, it kept cropping up—in Tena—in Dan English—in Si Booth.

He finished his breakfast, paid for it and went out to the walk again. He glanced across at the Buckhorn. The Grego brothers were probably in a mean mood this morning. They'd spent a night in jail. Chuck, with his arm broken, probably hadn't slept at all.

Morgan was willing to bet all three of them were drinking heavily. And that Sam, his father, was drinking with them.

In that combination was the potential explosiveness of the situation. Drunk, or even partly so, the Grego brothers might talk too much. Sam would be listening. And if Sam Orr got wind of what had happened to Rossiter, or suspected that the bank was in trouble, it would be all over town in less than an hour.

Thoughtfully, he returned to the hotel and found himself a chair on the veranda. He had been there only long enough to roll and smoke a cigarette when the lobby door opened and Lily Leslie came out onto the veranda.

Her smile was sheepish and a trifle worried. 'I overslept. I always do on Sunday.'

Morgan got courteously to his feet. 'You were up half the night taking care of me and—' he looks at his clean clothes—'doing this.'

She smiled. 'I didn't do it. I gave them to the hotel chambermaid. She washed and ironed them for you.'

He gestured toward a chair. 'Sit down for a while. Or are you on your way to church?'

'No. I don't go to church. I'm not welcome there.'

She sat down and Morgan followed suit. It was almost nine o'clock.

He saw Dan English come around the corner. Dan stood for a moment on the corner, looking up and down the street. There was a tension in him very apparent to Morgan Orr, who was familiar with such things. The sheriff hitched at his gun and looked purposefully toward the Buckhorn.

Morgan called, 'Dan.'

The sheriff, swinging his head, saw Morgan and Lily on the porch, turned and came toward

94

them. As he mounted the steps, he pulled his big silver watch from his vest pocket and looked at it.

Morgan asked, 'Did you give them a deadline for getting out of town?'

The sheriff glanced at him, startled. 'How did you know?'

'I guessed. Be careful, Dan. They've been in the Buckhorn ever since it opened at eight o'clock. Sam's with them.'

Lily's face was concerned. She asked, 'Are you in trouble, Dan?'

'No trouble,' he replied heavily, not meeting her eyes.

Morgan felt a sudden kinship for the sheriff. Whatever Dan did from here on out would be wrong. Because he'd started wrong. He could run the Grego brothers out of Arapaho Wells, but he couldn't keep them out. And he couldn't keep the lid on a secret like the one he was trying to suppress. Sooner or later someone was going to let things slip...

Dan's face said he knew this. Morgan pulled his legs under him. 'Want me to go along?'

Dan shook his ponderous head slowly. 'That'd be the worst thing I could do. That would trigger them for sure. But thanks just the same.'

He tipped his hat to Lily and turned to go. Morgan watched him silently, fully aware that Dan's appearance in the Buckhorn might well be answered with a burst of gunfire that would shatter the peace of this Sunday morning and begin the chain of events which would wreck the town and all the people in it.

Lily's hand touched Morgan's arm. 'Go with him. Please.'

He glanced at her, but she wasn't looking at him. Her eyes were upon Dan English's broad back as he strode along down the street. There was softness in them, tenderness that was unmistakable. Lily Leslie was a woman in love and this morning it showed.

Morgan shook his head. 'I'd like to, but I can't. He may be able to handle them if I'm not there. If I was there, he wouldn't have a chance. I broke Chuck's arm last night. I smashed Al's nose. The sight of me would be like waving a red flag at a bull.'

Her face was pale. Her eyes shifted back to Dan English, who now was entering the saloon. He passed from sight.

Morgan caught himself listening intently. Lily was obviously doing the same thing. His hand went out and touched hers. It was damp and cold. He said reassuringly, 'Dan will be all right.'

'I hope so. Oh God, I hope so!'

Morgan asked, 'Does he know how you feel about him?'

She flushed. 'Yes.'

'Does he feel the same way?'

She avoided his eyes. 'I think he does.'

'Then what's holding him back?'

'Don't you know?'

He shook his head.

There was bitterness in her face now, a smoldering anger in her eyes. 'It's the label. Do you think he could stay in Arapaho Wells if he married me? Do you think those upstanding churchgoers would let him stay? Do you think he'd ever win another election?'

Morgan was thinking that Dan English would never win another election anyway. Dan English was through as sheriff here. Once the story of Rossiter was known.

He said, 'Don't give up. Something may happen. I think Dan is going to need you before long.'

Her eyes filled instantly with fear. She half rose in her chair. 'You mean now? You mean today?'

He pulled her back. 'No. Not today. I doubt if it will be today.'

But he wasn't sure. There was a feel in the air of the town, a feel he knew now was not entirely his own imagination.

CHAPTER TEN

Seemingly the town drowsed in the bright autumn sunlight of this peaceful Sunday morning. From the church up the street came the sound of the organ, and the blended voices

97

of the congregation.

Morgan's eyes were glued to the entrance of the Buckhorn, his ears tuned and strained for the sound of shouts, or gunshots. Beside him, Lily also stared at the Buckhorn, her face pale, her lips moving soundlessly.

Down there, the door opened. Al Grego came out, followed by Chuck. Curt brought up the rear.

The door banged shut behind them. They stood in a little group, talking, for several minutes. From their attitudes, Morgan guessed they were arguing.

At last, however, they turned away and headed for Si Booth's livery barn.

Still Morgan and Lily watched silently. The sheriff did not reappear. Lily asked breathlessly, 'Do you think they've hurt him?'

Morgan shook his head. 'He's staying inside until they've gone. Crowding them wouldn't be smart right now. Dan knows better than to do it.'

Still arguing, Chuck and Al and Curt stood waiting in the stable archway. After a few minutes, Morgan saw Si Booth lead their horses out. Without paying him, they swung astride and rode into the street.

Morgan knew he ought to get up and go inside. He knew they'd ride past the hotel and knew as well that sight of him would offer them release from their angry frustration.

But he couldn't move—or wouldn't. A

strong sense of pride prevented it, coupled with an even stronger instinct for self-preservation. They couldn't fail to see him if he got up and went inside. They'd know they had him on the run, an advantage they'd be sure to follow up at the first opportunity.

He turned his head. 'Get inside, Lily. Quick.'

She didn't argue, or even protest. She got up quickly and went inside.

Morgan leaned back comfortably and put his booted feet up on the rail. He looked relaxed, even indolent, but it was a deceptive thing. Inside him every nerve was screaming, every muscle tight. He was unarmed, and would have no chance if they decided to murder him as he sat here on the porch. But it would have to be murder. He'd give them no excuse for claiming they thought he had a gun.

They rode abreast, in the exact middle of the street. There was an unpredictable wildness about them that Morgan could almost smell. All three watched him steadily. Then, as though at a signal, they wheeled their horses, rode to him and stopped.

All had been drinking heavily, a circumstance that would tend to make them more reckless, more unthinking of consequences. Morgan put his eyes on Chuck, the acknowledged leader of the three, even though he knew Curt to be the most deadly. He didn't speak.

Chuck said nastily, 'Can't you get up?'

Morgan smiled, his eyes unwavering. He didn't reply, and he didn't move.

Chuck's face flushed with anger. 'God damn you, answer me!'

Morgan carefully and slowly reached for the tobacco in his shirt pocket. He selected a paper from the pack with elaborate care, and poured flake tobacco into the trough it made in his fingers. He licked it, twisted the ends and stuck it into his mouth. He said, 'Got a match, Chuck?'

For an instant he thought Chuck would burst a blood vessel. Chuck's face grew dark with congested blood. The veins on his forehead stood out in stark relief.

Beside him, Al reached in his pocket. He tossed Morgan a box of safety matches. Morgan caught them and said shortly, 'Thanks,' without removing his eyes from Chuck.

Curt said softly, 'Come on, Chuck. There'll be another time.' There was no fear in Curt's voice, no uncertainty in his pale eyes.

Morgan shifted his glance to Curt. He was surprised to see no hate in Curt, only that cold, steady promise.

No bluster in this one, he thought. No empty threats. Just the promise in his eyes, not of a fight which either could win, but of death. Curt wouldn't care how he accomplished it. Rules were for other men, not for Curt.

Chuck reined reluctantly away. The others

followed. From the center of the street, Curt looked back.

Morgan lighted the cigarette, and stared at Curt over the flame of the match. Their glances locked and held.

Then Curt turned away. The three trotted up the street and out of town.

Morgan drew deeply on the cigarette. He looked at his hands, expecting to see them trembling. They were steady as a rock.

But his forehead was damp and his shirtback was soaked with sweat.

He saw Dan English step from the Buckhorn and walk toward him up the street. Lily Leslie came out of the hotel, her face white. She smiled shakily. 'I wish my knees would stop knocking together.'

Morgan looked up. 'They're gone, and everything's all right.'

Dan paced steadily up the street. Lily sat down in the rocker next to Morgan and began nervously to rock. The chair squeaked faintly as she did.

Dan's face was worried as he climbed the three veranda steps. Morgan studied him, and saw no relief in him. He asked, 'Sam still down in the Buckhorn?'

The sheriff nodded and said, with a careful oblique glance at Lily, 'Sam either knows something or has guessed it.' There was a vast discouragement in Dan English. His eyes were bleak, staring at the certainty that today his secret would be told, with inevitable, disastrous consequences. 'I should have run the Gregos out of town as soon as I let them out of jail. I should never have given them a chance to get liquored up.'

Lily's voice was soft. 'I don't understand. Are you in trouble, Dan?'

He frowned. 'I'm afraid I am.'

'Can I help?'

Morgan glanced at her. Her face was very soft. He wondered if Dan English fully appreciated her true value. He wondered if any man could ever fully appreciate it.

Dan shook his head, without even looking at Lily.

Lily stood up. 'All right, Dan.' She went inside.

Morgan scowled. 'You're a damned fool, Dan.'

Dan's temper flared. 'Is that your business?'

'No.'

The sheriff calmed himself with an effort. 'What kind of a man do you think I am? I wouldn't offer her a share of my life when it amounted to something. Do you think I'll offer it now, when it's about to fall apart?'

Morgan said softly, 'I doubt if she cares what you offer her, as long as you go with the deal.'

'You're the fool, Morgan. I'm forty-one years old. I'm a homely bastard, and Lily's a beautiful woman. I've got to give her

102

something more than just myself.'

Morgan shrugged. He said, 'All right, feel sorry for yourself if it helps any. But not everybody judges other people by their good looks or the money they've got in the bank.'

Dan English didn't answer. He stared moodily across the street at the bank.

Its blinds were drawn, its door padlocked. Morgan wondered if it would ever open again.

He said softly, 'Why don't you hustle Sam down to the jail and lock him up? Before he talks?'

For a time the sheriff didn't answer. He seemed to be considering Morgan's suggestion. Then he shook his head. 'Maybe I don't want to put it off any longer. I guess I'm kind of glad it's coming out.'

Up the street the church organ, which had been silent, again began to play. The voices of the congregation joined with it, to sing a hymn vaguely familiar to Morgan, probably from his boyhood. The sound rolled along the street and then, abruptly, stopped.

Dan English muttered, 'It won't be long now.'

'Get Sam out of the way. Lock him up. Give yourself time to plan what you're going to do. It's not too late to arrest Jerome and the Gregos.'

'And save myself?'

'What's wrong with that?'

'Nothing maybe. I don't know. Only I won't

do it.'

Morgan watched the people stream from the door of the church. They clustered briefly on the steps and the walk. Then they began to disperse, some walking, some disappearing behind the church and reappearing after several minutes driving buggies or buckboards.

A number of the men left their families and headed toward the two saloons at the lower end of town. The street was briefly filled, then slowly it began to empty.

A sleepy, quiet day. On the surface. Morgan realized his body was as tense as it had been while the Gregos sat their horses staring down at him.

He thought of Tena, and of her daughter Serena—his daughter too. He said, 'Damn it, Dan, you'd better get Jerome in jail. For his own safety.'

For the first time, Dan English seemed uncertain. He looked down toward the Buckhorn, then upstreet in the direction of Mel Jerome's house. He said, 'I don't know.' He got ponderously, wearily to his feet. 'I'm going down there. Anything's better than sitting here waiting.'

'Want me to go with you?'

The sheriff shook his head. 'I can handle it better alone.' He got up and went heavily down the steps to the street. He walked along it toward the Buckhorn Saloon, a man who had filled his office well for fifteen years, but who, at last, had made the mistake no lawman could afford—that of interpreting his responsibilities instead of carrying them out to the letter of the law.

Morgan watched him thoughtfully. He got up stiffly and paced back and forth on the hotel veranda. He wished he hadn't sold his gun. Something told him he was going to need it before this day was done.

Knowledge of Rossiter's killing and the bank's difficulties might take the town's mind off Morgan Orr temporarily. But he was involved. He couldn't stand by and see Tena hurt. He wouldn't stand by and let the town wreak its violent vengeance on the man she was married to.

Jerome would have to stand trial for Rossiter's death, along with the Gregos, but it had to be a trial, not the vengeance of a mob.

In spite of the warmth of the day, Morgan's body suddenly felt cold.

*   *   *

Dan English stepped into the Buckhorn and stopped inside the door. Sam Orr stood at the bar, a bottle and glass before him.

He was very drunk. His eyes were bloodshot, his jaws unshaven and covered with a grayish, untidy stubble.

There were about a dozen men in the saloon

with Sam, and all were clustered around him at the bar.

One of them, Carl Roushe, who ran a grocery store, called to Dan English, 'Sheriff, come here. You remember that little bank examiner that was here six months ago? Sam says the Gregos killed him.'

Dan crossed the room. He looked at Sam Orr with dislike that amounted to disgust.

Carl Roushe said, more softly, 'He says you knew about it, Dan.'

Dan fixed Roushe with his eyes. 'And you believe him?'

'I didn't say that,' Roushe replied defensively.

The sheriff stared at Sam Orr. 'Let's have the story, Sam.'

Sam sneered openly. 'Whadda ya mean, let's have the story? You son of a bitch, you know the story. Rossiter was murdered by the Gregos.'

The sheriff stared coldly at him. 'Got proof of it, Sam?'

'Proof? He disappeared, didn't he?'

Roushe broke in. 'Why'd they kill him, Sam? *If* they did.'

Sam's face flushed angrily. 'If, hell! They did, I tell you.'

'Did they rob him? Was that why?'

Sam laughed mockingly. He said, 'Use your head. Rossiter was a bank examiner. He spent his last day on earth in Jerome's bank. Figure it

106

out for yourselves.'

He picked up the bottle in front of him and drank from it as though it were water. His prominent adams apple bobbed in his scrawny neck with each swallow.

Roushe seized the bottle and yanked it away from him. 'God damn you, Sam, you're not going to make an accusation like this and then drink yourself unconscious before you can explain it!'

But he was already too late. Sam's eyes were glazing.

Dan English looked at Sam with disgust, then at the faces of the men around him.

He saw several things in their faces—fear—confusion—puzzlement. He caught Roushe looking at him speculatively. Roushe said coldly, 'What about it, sheriff?'

Dan met his eyes steadily, 'What about what?'

'Sam's made an accusation. A serious one. Aren't you going to do anything about it?'

Dan said, 'I'll check it out.' Now that the time had arrived to confess his guilty knowledge, he found he couldn't do it. He liked these men. He had served them faithfully for fifteen years. He couldn't bear to see contempt for him in their eyes.

Roushe said with sudden, furious sarcasm, 'You'll check it out? When? For Christ's sake, man, what's the matter with you? A man disappears completely from the face of the earth. Someone says he's been murdered, and even tells you who did it. And you say you'll check it out!'

Dan swung, white-faced. 'You want to ride today?'

'You're damned right we want to ride! Today and tomorrow and all next week if that's what it takes to find out what this is all about!'

Dan's body seemed to settle. He said, 'All right. Go change your clothes. Saddle your horses. Load your guns. I need about ten men for a posse.'

The men began to disperse. Dan spoke again. 'Two or three of you stay here. Take Sam out and dunk him in the horse trough. Pour coffee into him. I want a straight story out of him before we move.' Before he had finished speaking he realized he was unconsciously stalling for time. And he knew it was useless.

He could see excitement beginning to rise in the men. They streamed out the door, two of them carrying Sam, who protested drunkenly.

The sheriff stood there for a moment, then walked to the door. Several of the men were running up the street. They shouted back and forth with other men on the walks. The town began to come alive.

So far, he thought, things were orderly enough. So far, the town was motivated only by righteous anger over a murder they believed had been committed in their town.

But Dan English had seen these things before. Excitement would possess the men for a while. Maybe he could keep them under control and take the Gregos without undue violence.

But the words of Sam Orr, a drunken, lying bum, were one thing—the words of the three Grego brothers quite another. When the Gregos spilled what they knew to the posse, when the men of the town began to be touched personally by this, they would begin to change.

They might very well demand that Jerome open his bank, even though it was Sunday. When he refused ... Dan shook his head. He didn't want to think about that.

He knew one thing—it was going to be up to him and him alone to see that the town remained orderly. And he wondered if he could. When they found out he had known of the bank's difficulties and Rossiter's murder all along...

Respect for the law, which Dan English personified, would disappear, and lawlessness would take its place. When that occurred Arapaho Wells would become a town without reason, a town ruled only by the mob.

Sam Orr was dumped unceremoniously into the horse trough down beside the livery barn. He came up, soaked, spluttering, mouthing obscenities. Dan turned and walked up the street to the corner. Without looking at

Morgan Orr on the porch of the hotel, he rounded it and walked swiftly to his office.

He did not go in. He went instead to the shed behind the jail where he kept his horse and began to saddle up, unable to steady his trembling hands.

CHAPTER ELEVEN

Morgan Orr sat motionless on the hotel veranda, listening to the town come alive. Sensitive through long experience to the changing moods of many towns, he felt the change in this one almost as strongly as he would have felt a change in temperature or an impending storm.

No longer was the menace hovering over Arapaho Wells vague and mostly a thing of instinct within himself. Now it was tangible.

Excitement came first; it always did. Life was dull and things like manhunts and posses tended to liven it up. But the ride out to the Grego ranch was a long one and excitement would inevitably wear off. Then the men would begin to think.

Meanwhile, those left in town would be thinking too. They would begin to reason that if Rossiter had been murdered, there had to have been a reason for it.

So far, there had been no mention of Jerome

or the bank—at least in the shouts and conversation Morgan had been able to overhear. Maybe his father had been too drunk to tell his story straight. Maybe Sam hadn't connected Rossiter's murder with possible difficulties in the bank.

But if he had . . . They were sobering him up right now by dunking him in the horse trough at the livery barn.

Morgan got up suddenly and headed for the livery barn. Maybe he could talk some sense into Sam. Maybe he could persuade Sam to do no more talking. It wasn't likely, but he owed it to everyone concerned to have a try.

There were three men working on Sam down at the livery barn. One of them was Roy Forette. Another was Jim Dillon, who ran the blacksmith shop. The third Morgan didn't know.

He walked swiftly, ignoring the pain the movement caused. He was breathing rapidly when he reached the livery barn.

Sam Orr sat on an overturned washtub that was half rusted through. His long hair straggled into his face, dripping. Little rivulets of water ran from the cuffs of his pants, making a pool of mud at his feet. He was shivering violently.

Jim Dillon, his tremendous shoulders straining at his neat Sunday suit, said unsympathetically, 'Open up and talk, Sam. You won't get another drink, or dry clothes either, until you do.'

Sam looked up furiously. 'You sons of bitches can go to hell! You can't treat me like this!'

'Why not, you goddam soak?' Dillon cuffed Sam alongside the head and knocked him off the tub. 'Now talk! We haven't got all day!'

Morgan wondered at the instinctive desire he had to take Jim Dillon on, to avenge the blow Dillon had struck Sam. He didn't care about Sam, who, though he was his father, had long ago forfeited any right to his respect.

Sam got up unsteadily, his clothes now muddy from the dust. He brushed his hands ineffectually on his wet pants.

Morgan stared at Dillon, at Forette and at the other man. He realized nothing he could say to them now would make any difference. But he heard himself saying, 'Keep your hands off him, Dillon.'

Dillon whirled, scowling. 'And you keep your goddam nose out of this.'

Morgan met Dillon's glance steadily, and after a moment Dillon looked down at the ground. Morgan switched his eyes to Forette. The speculation was stronger in Forette's eyes, the hesitation almost gone. Forette's body tensed, his mouth tightened and his eyes narrowed. His tongue came out and licked his lips, this being the only apparent sign of nervousness.

He said softly, 'You making this a family matter?'

'And if I am?'

Forette said, 'Give him your gun, Dillon.'

Dillon didn't move. Forette's voice was sharper, higher as he snapped, 'Damn it, do what I say!'

Dillon fumbled with the belt clasp. Morgan didn't speak. Without taking his eyes from Forette, he got a silver dollar out of his pocket and flipped it to Sam. 'Go get yourself a drink, Sam. And then get some dry clothes on.'

Sam caught the dollar expertly. He glowered at Morgan for a moment, looked from Morgan to the others. Choosing the lesser of two evils, he turned toward the Buckhorn.

Forette said deliberately, 'You arrogant bastard!'

Morgan flushed with anger. Out of a corner of his eye he could see the proffered gun and belt in Dillon's shaking hand. This was the sort of thing a man had to take when he put aside his gun. It left a bad taste in his mouth, but not nearly so bad a taste as killing Forette would leave.

Confidence was strong now in Forette's voice. 'Take it, damn you! You're supposed to be a real fast gun. Let's see how fast you are. I think you've slipped. I think I can take you.'

There was a sameness to this pattern that was repetitious in Morgan's ears. In the past, pride had dictated Morgan's actions.

Afterward, there had always been dull regret and pity for the lifeless body in the dust before him. This time it had to be different. If he were to succeed in staying here, pride must be the first thing he relinquished. He swung his head and looked at Dillon. His voice was harsh. 'Put it back on. I don't want it.'

He knew full well what he did when he refused to fight Forette. He relinquished pride and with it the tenuous thread of respect that stretched between the people of the town and himself. Others would challenge him now— others with less skill than Forette possessed. By degrading him they would add to their own sense of importance.

Yet he knew he could do nothing but what he was doing. A killing would alienate him completely, and insure his being driven out...

Forette's voice was mildly amazed. 'Chuck was right, then. You're scared. You've lost your guts.'

Sam Orr came staggering out of the Buckhorn. He stared owlishly at the four in front of the livery barn. He turned uptown, but Dillon called, 'Wait a minute, you!'

He started toward Sam. Morgan caught his sleeve. Dillon jerked his arm away, put his hand in the middle of Morgan's chest and pushed.

Morgan staggered back. Fury churned in his brain. This was, he knew, the direct result of his refusing to fight Forette.

Dillon lumbered toward Sam. Morgan

overtook him and whirled him around. 'You got what you wanted out of Sam. Now let him alone.'

His face was white with anger, his eyes blazing. Dillon started to fling him aside again, but something stopped him. He blustered, 'We didn't get all we wanted. I want to know why the Gregos killed Rossiter. Was it for money, or ...?'

Morgan interrupted coldly, 'Why don't you ask the Gregos? Or do you figure that might be more dangerous than badgering a drunk?'

Dillon sneered, 'Look who's talking!'

Morgan's eyes didn't waver. They held Dillon's steadily. Morgan murmured, 'Don't push too hard. Forette said I'd lost my guts, but that doesn't necessarily make it so.'

Dillon held his glance a moment more. At last he grumbled something indistinguishable and turned to the others. 'To hell with Sam. Let's get our horses and get out to the Gregos' place. We'll see what they've got to say.'

Morgan waited, his face without expression. Roy Forette was watching him. Letdown was apparent in Roy, as was the vaguest kind of disappointment. But there was something else, that Morgan couldn't define, in the slight smile on Forette's wide mouth.

Morgan scowled at him. In spite of what Forette had just done, he couldn't help liking Forette's youthful brashness and he didn't want to like Forette. He couldn't afford to. If

115

he was forced into a showdown with Roy, liking him was certain to affect the outcome.

Dillon and the other men headed up the street, with briefly puzzled glances at Morgan. Forette went into the livery barn.

The sheriff came around the corner, riding his buckskin horse. Morgan fished his tobacco from his pocket and rolled a smoke. His mouth twisted wryly. The town had hated him for the gun at his side, for the violence he might attract. Now they would hate him and hold him in contempt because he had backed down from Roy Forette.

A bit of inconsistency that was very human, he realized. But it wouldn't make things a damned bit easier for him.

Dan English rode up to him and sat looking down. He cleared his throat and finally asked, 'Would you mind going along, Morg? I . . .' He stopped, plainly angered by his own embarrassment.

Morgan waited, seeing the pride in Dan English, but needing salve for his own pride too. At last Dan said determinedly, 'I might need some help.'

Morgan was suddenly ashamed. If it hadn't been for Dan's help in the Buckhorn last night, he'd probably be dead. He said, 'Sure, Dan. Sure, I will.' He turned and entered the stable.

Forette was leading his horse out. He swung to the saddle in the archway, grinning down at Morgan. 'Goin' along for the fun? Be sure and

116

stay back out of range.'

Morgan frowned. 'Killings are never fun, boy, and you'll find out if you keep going the way you're headed.'

Forette flushed angrily at the word, 'boy.' He might have said something else, but Morgan turned away.

Si Booth was back in the alleyway between the stalls. Morgan said, 'Give me a good one, Si. The best you've got.'

Si nodded and turned away. He came out a few moments later leading a gleaming brown gelding. He saddled the prancing animal and Morgan swung up. The gelding ducked his head, but Morgan pulled it back up, his arm straining against the reins. He said, 'This is on the county, Si.'

'Sure. But you ain't goin' out unarmed, are you?'

'I'll get a rifle from Dan.'

He rode out into the street. The gelding kept trying to get his head, but Morgan wouldn't let him. The ride out to the Grego place would be hard enough, as sore as his body was, but riding a bucking horse would be a hell of a sight worse.

Along the street now, men were gathering. Half a dozen mounted men raced around the corner by the hotel and headed toward the sheriff's office.

Others, unmounted, began to gather curiously. Forette was waiting beside the sheriff, who said shortly, 'Let's go.'

Morgan followed the pair up the street, his eyes searching among those on the walks for Jerome or Tena. He saw neither of them. He wondered briefly if he was wise to accompany the sheriff, then decided that nothing would happen in town until the posse returned. Jerome and Tena would be safe enough. For now.

As they rode up to the sheriff's office, Morgan said, 'I'll need a rifle, Dan.'

Dan English dismounted. Forette grinned mockingly at Morgan and spoke to Dan. 'Don't give him one, Dan. He might get hurt.'

Morgan didn't speak. The assembled men were staring at him with plain dislike that was no longer tempered with fear. Dan English came out, carrying two rifles, one of which he handed up to Morgan along with a box of cartridges. He shoved the other into the boot on his saddle.

Jim Dillon said truculently, 'You ain't lettin' *him* come along, are you?'

Dan swung his head, 'Why not?'

'Because he ain't much better than the Grego bunch. If any.'

Dan English looked at Dillon dryly. 'You reckon he's any more bloodthirsty than the rest of you?'

Dillon flushed. 'You got no call to ...'

'Oh shut up!'

Dan English waited until all the men were

118

quiet, then he said, 'Raise your right hands.'

They did. Dan said, 'Do you swear to uphold the law to the best of your ability?'

They grumbled, 'We do,' in ragged unison. Dan mounted his horse. 'All right then. Let's go.'

Dan English led the way out of town. He rode up Second, turned at Main and took the same road out which Morgan had used coming in early yesterday morning.

Thinking of that, Morgan was amazed at all that had happened in hardly more than twenty-four hours.

There was no rifle boot on Morgan's saddle, so he held the rifle cradled in his arms. As he rode, he opened the box of cartridges and dumped it into his jacket pocket. Then he withdrew several cartridges and stuffed them, one by one, into the loading slot on the rifle.

For a while the men rode silently. But gradually they began to talk. Morgan heard Jim Dillon's voice, 'Why'n hell would the Gregos kill Rossiter? They didn't know him, and it don't look like a bank examiner would be carrying much money.'

Somebody grumbled an answer that Morgan didn't hear. Then Roy Forette said, 'Figure it out for yourself.'

Jim Dillon spoke again. 'What the hell do you mean by that?'

'Ask Carl Roushe.'

Dillon's voice raised, 'What about that, Carl?'

Roushe's voice was irritable. 'I don't know a damn thing more about it than you do.'

'You were there in the Buckhorn when Sam accused the Gregos.'

Roushe was silent. Morgan heard a scuffle of hoofs and turned his head. Dillon was spurring up beside Carl Roushe's horse.

Dillon insisted, 'What'd Sam say? Did the killin' have anything to do with the bank?'

It was several moments before Roushe answered. Then he said, 'Sam seemed to think it did—he said Rossiter had spent the day in Jerome's bank and for us to figure it out for ourselves.'

A low rumble went the length of the line of mounted men. Dan English swung his head and roared, 'Shut up, the whole damn bunch of you! We'll take the Gregos and throw 'em in jail. When that's done, there'll be time for figuring out why they did it.'

Again the silence. Then Jim Dillon shouted, 'Sheriff, how come *you* didn't figure out that Rossiter had been killed?'

Dan English scowled and stared straight ahead. He didn't answer.

Morgan swung his head and looked back along the line. Forette, directly behind him, was watching him with a mocking half smile on his lips. Behind Forette was Carl Roushe, a balding, middle-aged man who looked like what he was, a misplaced storekeeper who had no business here at all.

Behind Roushe was Jim Dillon, scowling blackly as he tried, with his limited intelligence, to figure out the various ramifications involved in Rossiter's killing. He was watching Dan English's back suspiciously as though he had guessed that Dan knew more then he was telling.

The plain was rolling, tawny in the morning sun. Off yonder to the left, Morgan saw a bunch of twenty or so horses grazing. Up ahead was the outline of the jackpine-covered hills within which lay the Grego ranch.

Dan English plodded his buckskin horse along with deliberate slowness, as though dreading what lay ahead.

Behind Morgan speculation went on. Dillon rumbled as though thinking aloud, 'If there was somethin' wrong in the bank, an' if that's why Rossiter was killed, then...'

The sheriff hipped around in his saddle. 'I told you to cut it out! Hell, you ain't even sure there's been a murder. You ain't even sure Rossiter's dead. All you got is the word of a whisky-soaked bum. Now let it lie!'

Morgan stared at Dan English with admiration. The sheriff sounded mighty convincing. But what if the Gregos talked? That wasn't going to be as easy to pass off as Sam Orr's drunken accusations.

They reached the hills and strung out as they climbed their horses through the fragrant pines. The sheriff still rode in the lead, with Morgan Orr immediately behind him.

Forette gigged his horse until its head was against the flank of Morgan's horse. He asked, 'What do *you* think, Morg?'

'About what?' Morgan frowned. He realized suddenly that to Forette, gunfighting was only a game of brag and bluff, without rancor.

'About this killin' the Gregos are supposed to have done.'

Morgan swung his head. 'Dan will arrest them. They'll have a trial. If they're guilty, they'll hang.'

Forette chuckled. 'If they're guilty, maybe they'll hang sooner than you think. Along with whoever hired 'em to kill Rossiter.'

'That's crazy talk.'

'Not so damn crazy. This whole thing has got a bad smell if you ask me. How come Rossiter was missing six months before anyone got wind of the notion he might've been murdered? And why would the Gregos be mixed up in it? Another thing. Why did the three of them try to kill you last night? And why did they hotfoot it over to Jerome's house this morning as soon as they got out of jail?'

Morgan turned his head and stared at Forette coolly. 'Why ask me? I just arrived in town yesterday morning. I don't know Jerome at all, and I've never even been inside the bank.'

'Then why did the Gregos jump you?'

Morgan shrugged and countered with a

question of his own. 'Why did you jump me?'

Forette flushed at that, and looked away. Faced with putting reasons for his action into words, he was confused. At last he said sullenly, 'You're supposed to be the fastest gun in the country. All a man would have to do to take your place...'

'Would be to kill me. Do you think you're faster than I am?'

'Strap on a gun and we'll damn soon find out!'

Morgan laughed mirthlessly. 'It never occurs to a man your age that he can die, does it? Other people, sure. They can die. But not you. What in hell ever gave you the idea you were immortal?'

'Don't push *me*. You backed down a while ago. You must've figured I was faster'n you or you wouldn't...'

'You're talking like a stupid goddam kid!' Morgan said disgustedly. 'Why do you think I came back to Arapaho Wells?'

'How the hell should I know?' Forette was angry, but he was sullen, too, like a boy who is being scolded, who feels at a disadvantage and is defiant because he does.

'I got sick of living like an animal. I got sick of men being afraid of me—of never being wanted, no matter where I went.'

'And it's different here?'

'Not yet. But I'll make it different. At least I'll try.'

He spurred his horse ahead, conscious of Roy Forette's eyes resting on his back. He wondered briefly if Forette wanted to be top gun badly enough to shoot him down from behind. Then he put the thought from his mind. Forette wasn't that kind. Maybe before he was through, he'd manage to crowd Morgan into a gunfight. But he'd do it openly, shielded by his youthful confidence that death was for other men and not for him.

He had refused Forette's challenge today. He might refuse it again. But if Forette was determined enough, he would hunt and probe until he found Morgan's weaknesses. Taunted with his relationship with Tena, Morgan knew he'd fight, even if he killed Forette, even if he died himself.

Clouds were drifting across the sun now, and a stiff wind had raised in the west. It was a chill wind, with a smell of frost in it.

Morgan shivered, not entirely from cold, then drew rein as he came up close behind the sheriff.

They were climbing a long draw now, in the bottom of which was a washout twelve or fifteen feet deep. The sheriff said, 'I don't know how well you remember this country, Morg, but the Grego place is about a mile and a half ahead—just on the other side of that saddle.'

'I know.' Morgan rode in silence for a moment, then asked, 'What are you going to do?'

'Surround 'em and give 'em a chance to surrender. If they won't do that, we'll go in after them.'

Morgan wondered how many of the Grego brothers would be taken alive—or even if any of them would. He studied the back of Dan English's head, and asked himself a question. How far would Dan go to keep his secret? He shook his head in angry disgust. Dan was the sheriff, not a killer. But the nagging doubt remained.

CHAPTER TWELVE

On the near side of the saddle's crest, Dan English reined in his horse. He turned to face his posse, straggling up the road. Morgan swung his head and looked at them.

There was a certain puzzlement in Forette's eyes that did not seem connected with the job at hand. Dillon, next to halt his horse, was sweating as hard as though he had climbed the grade afoot. His eyes were strangely dilated, whether by fear or excitement, Morgan couldn't tell. He kept licking his lips nervously.

Behind Dillon came Carl Roushe, looking unhappy and uncomfortable. Obviously, now that the fighting was at hand, Roushe was wishing he hadn't come at all. But he didn't look afraid. Just reluctant at the distasteful

125

business ahead.

Besides these three, there were seven others. Three of them Morgan recognized as having been among those who jumped him last night in the Buckhorn.

There was nothing in them now to make Morgan think of a mob. They were nervous, scared, trying to hide under bravado the fact that they were. One said, 'What the hell we waitin' for? Let's go get 'em!'

Dan English raised his hand. 'Shut up, all of you. Listen to me. I don't want any gunplay if it can be avoided. I want them all alive. If any of you shoots except in defense of his life, I'll jug you and charge you with murder.'

A voice whined protestingly, 'Whose side you on, for Christ's sake?'

'The side of the law.' Dan stared at the man who had spoken, then said briskly, 'Morg, you an' Forette and Dillon and Roushe go to the right. It'll bring you up behind the house. Get set up there where they can't see you. Spread out a little. Wait.' He turned to the others. 'Roark, you and Thompson stay here. The rest of you come with me. Don't let 'em get away, but don't shoot unless they try.'

He reined off and headed toward the left end of the saddle.

Morgan led off in the other direction. He kept well to the right so that when he topped the saddle, he was hidden behind another ridge.

126

He hesitated about giving orders, but when the men seemed to want to stay bunched up, he said, 'Roushe, you drop off first.'

Roushe stopped, dismounted and tied his horse. Carrying a rifle he began to walk through the stunted jackpines toward the crest of the ridge to his left.

Morgan rode another eighth of a mile and said, 'Forette.'

Forette stopped, tied his horse and walked to a point from which he could see the ranch below.

It left Dillon and Morgan. Morgan hadn't liked the look in Dillon's eyes, and wanted the man where he could see him. He rode on and after a few minutes said tightly, 'All right, Dillon.'

Dillon glared at him defiantly. 'I'll go where I damn well please. I'm not taking orders from you.'

Morgan said evenly, 'Get off your horse.' As he spoke, he reined almost imperceptibly toward the man. Dillon made a move toward the gun at his side and Morgan swung his rifle unhesitatingly, almost instinctively.

The butt of it thumped against Dillon's chest, which echoed hollowly like a big bass drum. Wind drove out of Dillon explosively as he tumbled out of his saddle.

Morgan was on the ground even as Dillon struck it. He rounded the horses running.

Dillon, gagging and gasping on the ground,

yanked his revolver from its holster. He lifted it toward Morgan Orr, his face contorted with pain and hate.

Morgan kicked and the gun went spinning. Dillon cried out, and held his hurt hand against his chest.

Holding his rifle in the crook of his right arm, Morgan fished his sack of Durham from his pocket. He carefully rolled a cigarette, twisted its ends and stuck it in his mouth. He lighted it.

Dillon was breathing evenly again now, but his face looked sick. Though his eyes hated Morgan, the quality of cruel anticipation was gone from them. Morgan said softly, 'Get on up the hill.'

Dillon struggled to his feet and shot a glance toward his revolver where it lay a dozen feet away.

'Leave that,' said Morgan, 'until you come back for your horse.'

Sullenly Dillon shambled up the rise. He was a big man, almost as powerful as Al Grego, made so by the blacksmith work he did. But he was slow, of mind and body both.

Morgan stepped on his cigarette, mounted and rode on. He found himself a place from which he could see, not only the Grego place below, but Dillon on his left.

It was peaceful down below. A slatternly-looking woman was hanging wash out on a rickety clothesline strung between the house

128

and a couple of cedar poles. A couple of hogs rooted in front of the kitchen door in a puddle of soapsuds and garbage flung there earlier. Otherwise there was no sign of life, except in the corral, where three horses drowsed.

Morgan caught movement on the far ridge, and a moment later saw the form of Dan English ride above its crest. Dan bellowed, his voice lifting and carrying across the valley floor, 'Hello, the house! This is the sheriff! Come out with your hands up!'

The woman stopped hanging clothes, stared uncomprehendingly up at the sheriff for a moment. Then she dropped her armful of wet clothes in the dust and scuttled for the house.

For nearly five minutes, there was no sound. Dan English stood on the opposite ridge, legs spread, a plain, unmoving target. Morgan could almost tell what was going on in the sheriff's mind. At the moment, Dan didn't care if the Gregos shot him down or not. He was trapped and could see no way of getting clear.

Then Dan bellowed again, 'Chuck! Curt! Al! Get out of there. You're surrounded.'

The shack might have been deserted, for all the response he got. Morgan heard Dillon grumbling on his left, 'Goddam sons of bitches! I'll bet I could move 'em out of there!'

Clouds had now fully obscured the sun. The wind, blowing from the west, had a smell of frost and snow. And there in the west, clouds hung low and black against the horizon.

Morgan knew a storm was coming. Somehow, the lack of sunlight, the chilling air, those ominous clouds in the west, only intensified his feeling of foreboding. This would be a black Sunday for Arapaho Wells, one that would long be remembered with shame.

Suddenly a rifle cracked down there at the shack. A bullet kicked up dust less than a yard from Dan English's widespread feet. Dan jumped, ran back a few feet and flopped.

Instantly, Dillon's rifle to Morgan's left opened up. Dillon emptied it at the kitchen windows. When its reverberating boom died away, Morgan heard the tinkle of broken glass down below at the shack.

Morgan cursed softly under his breath. For he heard another sound, so faint he could almost believe he imagined it. It was the whimpering sound of a hurt woman.

Suddenly anger overcame him. He eased back until he was out of sight of the shack, then got up and ran toward the place where Dillon was. Something was jumping in his belly, half nausea, half terrible rage, at the senselessness of what Dillon had done.

Dillon heard him coming, rolled, and sat up, bringing his rifle to bear. Morgan's voice was cold with fury. 'Go ahead, you son of a bitch! Shoot it or throw it away. Because if you don't, I'm going to bend it over your stupid damned head!'

130

Dillon pulled the trigger, but the gun only made an empty click. Dillon levered it frantically, and pulled the trigger again. Again it clicked.

Then Morgan was on him. Morgan's boot, its wild swing driven by unthinking anger, struck Dillon in his mouth.

The blacksmith was bowled back, and lost his rifle as he rolled. Morgan stopped, and stared at the man disgustedly for a moment. Then, while Dillon lay there on the ground wiping at his smashed mouth with the back of a hand, Morgan stooped, picked up his rifle, and flung it as far as he could downhill in the direction of the shack. It landed on the slope, fully exposed, and a hundred feet away.

He said, 'You'll have to go after it before you can use it again, and I doubt if you've got the guts for that. Know what you've done? You've hit that woman of Chuck's. Now, by God, they'll fight to the last man.'

He turned his back and stalked away. He returned to his previous position, his anger fading now. All he remembered about Dillon was the burning intensity of his eyes as he lay there wiping his bloody mouth.

Below, at the shack, a rifle opened up from one of the smashed kitchen windows. Bullets ricocheted on the slope and whined away. Two more rifles opened up from the front of the house, and across the way, members of the sheriff's posse opened up with theirs, firing

131

indiscriminately and in complete disregard of the sheriff's specific orders.

Faintly, Morgan could hear Dan English's angry bellowing, but it had no effect. On his left, he heard Dillon open up with his revolver, which he had apparently recovered. The range was too long and it was doubtful if he'd hit anything, so Morgan paid no heed.

Meanwhile, the shack was being riddled by bullets which tore through its flimsy walls as though they were paper. And the hurt woman continued to weep and scream, in a panic of terror and pain.

Suddenly Morgan could stand no more. He had no liking for the Gregos, and knew they had killed Rossiter without mercy. Still they were men, not wolf pups to be exterminated as such. And the woman, Chuck's wife, had done nothing.

He got up and ran for his horse. He mounted and pounded back in the direction he had come. There was a blind side to the shack, that faced the saddle. Going in on the blind side of the house might be dangerous, particularly for Morgan whom the townspeople liked no better than they did the Gregos, but it was a chance he had to take. He wasn't going to lie here helplessly until everyone in the shack was dead.

Three of the members of the posse had been among those who had attacked him in the Buckhorn last night. Dillon hated him enough to shoot him down. He realized these things, but did not slow down.

Passing the spot where Roy Forette was stationed, Morgan realized that Forette was among the few who were not shooting. But beyond him, Roushe was firing steadily, stopping only long enough to reload.

Morgan swung right onto the saddle, which was covered thickly with scrub jackpine. When he reached the center, its lowest spot, he wheeled and raced toward the shack.

He heard Dillon's thick voice clearly, even over the sporadic rifle shots and the pound of his horse's hoofs. 'He's goin' to join 'em. Cut the bastard down!'

And the sheriff's bellow, 'Stop firin'! Damn it, hold your fire!'

Morgan, his horse at a hard gallop, raced up to the blind side of the shack, dismounted and hit the ground running. As he came around the corner of the shack, his rifle at ready, the front door opened, and Chuck Grego came staggering out.

Blood streamed down the side of his face from a deep gash on his temple. He held his rifle cradled against his body by his splintered right arm, steadied by his left hand on the barrel.

He did not see Morgan, but fired blindly at the unseen men on the ridge. His face was contorted, his eyes wild.

Morgan heard the sodden sound of a bullet striking him, and saw him driven back a step as though struck by a giant fist. The rifle clattered from Chuck's hands. He stood, numbed and shocked for a moment, then quietly crumpled toward the ground. As he fell, another bullet struck him in the face. Its force jerked his head back and tore on through, taking a chunk out of the back of his head.

In that instant, Morgan hated the members of the posse who had fired those shots far more than he hated the Gregos. There was a kind of hysteria in the members of the posse that made them keep shooting at Chuck, even though he was dead and motionless on the ground. Bullets kicked up spurts of dust around him.

Morgan had seen similar hysteria directed against a mad dog; he had seen it last night in the Buckhorn, directed against himself.

Chuck's running out, his dying and falling had happened in the space of a few seconds, while Morgan rounded the corner of the shack, ran across the intervening space to the door and burst inside.

His eyes took in the scene instantaneously. Al lay spread-eagled by one of the windows, his hair and the side of his face soaked with blood.

The woman, Chuck's wife, moaned softly from a far corner of the room where she crouched like a hurt animal. Curt was not in sight.

Morgan heard a rifle boom in the next room, the kitchen, and heard it boom again. The whole inside of the house was filled with acrid powder smoke, and he felt like coughing.

He restrained himself determinedly and walked silently toward the kitchen door.

Curt knelt at the left side of the window, apparently unhurt. He was resting his rifle on the window jamb, sighting at something up on the hill behind the house.

As Morgan stepped in, he fired. Morgan crossed the room in a frantic lunge, counting on time, the time it would take Curt to turn, the time it would take him to jack another cartridge into the chamber of his rifle.

He swung his rifle as he lunged, reached Curt just as the man began to turn, and brought the rifle barrel solidly down on the top of Curt's head.

Curt sagged, his rifle clattering from his hands. He folded over sideways and came to rest stretched out below the window sill.

Morgan wondered briefly if he'd done the right thing. If he'd let the posse go ahead, if he'd let them butcher all three of the Gregos, then Dan English's secret would have remained a secret. With Curt alive, that was impossible.

And yet he knew this was the way Dan wanted it. Dan had given strict orders to his posse that there should be no unnecessary shooting or killing. He had tried desperately to stop them even after the shooting began.

Morgan crossed to the front door and stepped outside. He raised both hands and waved them back and forth. Then he beckoned and shouted, 'Come on in, Dan. It's all over!'

A bullet tore through the wall of the shack at his side. He flinched, but held his ground. He heard Dan shouting furiously up on the crest of the ridge, a moment later saw the sheriff come riding over it, spurring his horse with visible movements of his legs like those of a bronc rider at a county fair.

Dan thundered recklessly down the slope and dismounted running, as Morgan had done. He skidded to a halt at Morgan's side, his eyes switching to Chuck's mutilated body a dozen feet away. His horse, smelling blood, snorted and trotted away, dragging the reins.

Dan said anxiously, 'All of them Morg?'

Morgan shook his head. 'I slugged Curt. Other than that, I don't think Curt's hurt at all.'

'Chuck's wife?'

Morgan shook his head again. 'She's still alive. I don't know how bad she's hurt.'

Dan English went inside, and Morgan followed. Dan approached Mrs Grego gently. Morgan went into the kitchen to make sure Curt was still unconscious. He was. Morgan picked up his rifle and revolver and returned with them to the other room.

Dan was carrying Mrs Grego to the couch. On the floor, where she had lain was a pool of congealing blood.

Dan's face was sick. The members of the posse came trooping in the door. Dan stood up

136

and turned to face them furiously. 'Get out of here. God damn you, get out!'

They backed off, cowed by the intensity of his voice, by his blazing eyes. Grumbling, they went on out the door. In the front yard, their protesting voices rose, justifying what they had done, sourly criticizing the sheriff for his anger.

Morgan said softly, 'Will she die, Dan?'

Dan rose from where he had been kneeling beside the couch. 'She's already dead.'

Morgan was reminded fleetingly of his thoughts a while ago up on the hill behind the house. A black Sunday to be long remembered with bitter shame. And it wasn't over yet.

CHAPTER THIRTEEN

For a few moments they stood there silently. Morgan's eyes traveled from the pool of blood where Mrs Grego had lain, back through the doorway into the kitchen, following the erratic trail she had left as she crawled along the floor.

The sheriff's voice was lifeless and without expression. 'Who was it that opened up on the house? Dillon?'

Morgan nodded.

He heard sound in the kitchen, and a moment later Curt Grego staggered into the doorway. His eyes went first to Al, still spread-eagled on the floor. Confusedly they switched across the room to the couch on which Chuck's wife lay. He looked at Dan English then, and said almost dazedly, 'Chuck?'

'He's dead, too!'

There was concentrated virulence in Curt's voice. 'You dirty son of a bitch!'

Dan's face flushed angrily. 'I gave you a chance to surrender.'

Curt didn't reply. He stared at Morgan Orr, his eyes deadly and filled with hate. 'You started all this.'

Morgan shrugged. Nothing would be accomplished by arguing. He said, 'I'll saddle their horses, Dan.'

Dan English shook his head. 'Wait. Harness up a team. Hitch up the wagon. Just saddle a horse for Curt.'

Morgan nodded and went outside. He could feel the hostile eyes of the posse members on his back as he crossed the yard, and smiled sourly to himself. They were ashamed and aghast at the sudden carnage here. They were hunting a goat, upon which they could heap the blame for the wrong they had committed themselves.

Morgan shivered slightly as he walked across the yard. He glanced skyward and saw the sun, luminous and barely visible through the thin layer of driving clouds overhead. Good God, he thought, was it only noon? It seemed like a month since they'd ridden out of Arapaho Wells. It seemed like a year since he'd ridden in, and that had only been yesterday morning.

He reached the corral and caught up three horses. He tied one to the fence and led the other two across the yard to the Gregos' light spring wagon. The posse was grouped in front of the house.

Harness was draped on the wagon's sides. Morgan straightened it out and flung it on the horses, one by one. He put collars on, buckled the girths and after that hitched the tugs to the wagon singletrees. He climbed up on the seat and drove the wagon across the yard to the front door.

He returned to the corral and flung a weathered saddle onto the other horse. He led it back to the house.

Dan English and members of the posse were lifting the bullet-riddled bodies of Chuck Grego and his wife into the wagon bed. They laid Chuck on one side, his wife next to him, leaving space on the other side for Al. They went into the house for Al's body.

A shout raised, 'Hey! What the hell? He's gone!'

Morgan stood frozen for a moment. He'd have sworn Al was dead, but maybe he hadn't been. He must have crawled away—maybe into the kitchen.

He was startled by the drum of hoofs behind the house. He ran around it and saw Al, a hundred feet away, riding one of the possemen's horses. He started to raise his rifle, then let it drop back to his side.

Beside him, Dillon yelled, 'Shoot, damn you! Shoot!'

The range was now nearly a hundred yards. Al's horse lunged up the hill into the scattered cedars.

A shot blasted behind Morgan. Dust kicked up ahead of Al's horse. The horse swerved.

The possemen had recovered from their surprise. A volley of shots barked, but Al rode on, untouched. He rode out of sight into the cedars, and disappeared over the crest of the ridge.

Dillon asked accusingly, 'Why didn't you shoot? You could've got him easy!'

Morgan ignored him. Maybe Dillon hadn't got his belly full of killing, but Morgan had seen all he wanted to for one day. Al could be picked up later. Hurt as badly as he was, he couldn't travel far.

He returned to the front of the shack. Balding little Carl Roushe turned from his task of covering the two bodies with a blanket and ran around the side of the house. Morgan heard him retching. The others either glared at Morgan, or looked toward the place Roushe had disappeared, uneasiness in their grayish faces.

Morgan spoke to Dan. 'I'd have sworn he was dead.'

'Forget it. He won't go far. We'll get him.'

He glanced around at his posse. His eyes

140

settled on the blacksmith, Dillon. 'You drive the wagon.'

Dillon's face grew angry, but there was uneasiness and defiance in his eyes. 'Me? Why me? Ain't you goin' after Al?'

Dan's eyes snapped. 'That's my business, isn't it? You figuring on telling me how to run it?'

Dillon tried to hold the sheriff's eyes and failed. He grumbled something unheard by Morgan and climbed to the seat. Dan English shouted, 'All right! Get your horses and let's get going.'

Dillon drove the wagon out of the yard, taking the two-track road toward town. Morgan went around to the side of the house, got his horse and mounted. He rode in front and waited.

Dan looked at him speculatively and asked, 'Pretty good at followin' trail, Morg?'

'I get by.'

'Then get on Al's trail. See where it's headed. You can catch us before we get to town. Maybe it'll save a ride all the way back out here if we know where he's headed.'

Morgan nodded. He watched Dan English lead away, with Curt Grego riding sullenly beside him. Forette and the others strung out behind, shocked and silent now. Before they got to town, Morgan knew, they would begin to talk. Each would try to justify to the others the role he himself had played. But somewhere among these men, known only to themselves, were those who had shot Chuck down in front of the house. Among them were men who had fired into his limp body as it lay helpless on the ground.

Upon each individual rested a part of the responsibility for the death of Grego's wife. Certainly Dillon had shot her. But Dillon's bullet might not have been the fatal one.

He turned and rode toward the ridge, following the trail of Al Grego's horse. He topped the ridge and entered the cedars.

Al had ridden hard, straight away from the cabin, for more than half a mile. Then his horse had stopped. Morgan saw the marks of the plunging animal's hoofs as he turned around and around, nervous and excited under Al's hard hand on the reins. Then his trail lined out straight in the direction of town, but traveling more slowly now.

Al had sat there, hurting, watching to see if the posse was on his trail. Finding that they were not, and needing help, he'd turned toward town, aware he'd get help no place else. Maybe he even intended to turn himself in. That depended, Morgan supposed, on how badly he was hurt. He might even be thinking, in his slow-witted way, of revenge for the deaths of Chuck and Chuck's wife.

Morgan rode back to the cabin, fast, and took the trail of the sheriff and his posse. Riding hard, he overtook them before they had gone more than three miles.

Dan glanced at him questioningly and he said, 'Lined out toward town.'

Dan frowned, and didn't reply. But he did step up his pace slightly and Morgan knew he was thinking, as Morgan had, that perhaps Al was thinking of revenge.

He glanced at Roy Forette. Roy's face was gray, his eyes sick. Morgan opened his mouth to speak, then closed it abruptly without doing so. Forette was learning. He had seen violence and death today and it had sickened him. Morgan hoped the impression made on Forette was strong enough to change the course of his life.

They had ridden almost a mile before Roy turned to him and spoke. 'Why the hell should it bother me like this?'

Morgan smiled bleakly. 'Look around at the others. It bothers them too.'

'But the Gregos were killers.'

'Were they? Did a judge and jury say they were? And what about Chuck's wife? I doubt if she ever killed anything bigger than a chicken.'

'That was an accident.'

Morgan looked at Roy steadily. 'Was it?'

Roy swallowed. 'No. I guess it wasn't an accident. If everybody had done what Dan told them to . . .'

Morgan softened. 'Don't blame yourself too much. You didn't even fire a shot.'

'But I was there. I watched it happening and

didn't try to stop it.'

'Nobody could have stopped it. Dan tried and so did I. It happened just the same.'

Roy studied his face. For the first time, Morgan failed to feel that calculated challenge in Forette's thoughts. Forette spoke almost as though he were thinking aloud. 'It isn't over.'

'No.' And it wasn't. The tendency of each posse member to find a goat for his own guilt would lead to more violence and more guilt. Morgan hoped Curt Grego would have sense enough to remain silent about Jerome, and Jerome's Arapaho Wells Bank. He doubted if Curt would, though. Curt was stunned now, but that would wear away. When it did, he would want to strike out at those who had hurt him. The most effective way of striking out at them would be to tell them about the bank.

They jogged along leisurely, mostly silent, but as the miles fell behind, gradually the men began to talk softly among themselves. Gradually, too, their voices began to rise, until they carried the length of the column.

Morgan heard Len Slaughter's rough, heavy voice say, 'What the hell's the matter with everybody? All we done was shoot back. They fired first.'

Another said, 'Chuck should have sent his woman out if he intended to make a fight of it. Hell, he might've known she'd catch a stray.'

Ahead of Morgan, Curt Grego swung his head. The impact of his eyes, so filled with concentrated hate, was almost like a physical shock to Morgan. He glanced on past Morgan to those behind. He said in a low voice that nevertheless carried to the end of the column, 'Chuck didn't intend to make a fight of it. Al fired that shot, and it would have killed the sheriff if Chuck hadn't hit him as he fired.'

He looked from one man to another. His voice was laden with contempt. 'So don't try to make it anything but exactly what it is— murder.' His lip curled. 'You damn stinkin' hypocrites! Some of you have still got your churchgoin' clothes on. But you're nothin' but killers, hidin' behind the sheriff's badge.'

Carl Roushe yelled, 'Make him shut up, Dan. Damn it, shut him up!'

Dan English didn't turn his head. Something about the tenseness of his back told Morgan he knew what was coming now. Curt Grego was going to spill the whole story.

He was tense himself. He knew men, and was sure the posse members would seize upon the information that the bank was broke as further justification for what they had done, for what they would do when they got back into town.

He also realized that he, Dan English, and Curt might not even get back to town alive. Because whatever happened he had to stand with Dan. Dan was all the law there was in Arapaho Wells. He was all the protection Jerome and Tena would have against the town.

Curt jogged along in silence for a while.

145

When he turned his head, there was a little, triumphant smile on his thin, cruel mouth.

'You're all so damned sure we killed Rossiter. But does any of you know why?'

Morgan said, 'Slug him, Dan. Don't let him...'

Forette said, 'Wait. Let him talk. I want to hear this.'

Dan English said, 'Think before you talk, Curt. Anything you say can be used against you.'

Curt laughed harshly. 'You think I care? I haven't got the chance of a snowball in hell of comin' out of this alive. So I'd just as well take the one that's really guilty with me.'

He waited. Silence along the column was virtually complete. Curt said, 'Sure. We killed Rossiter. He's buried in the middle of our corral. We got paid to do it.'

'Who paid you?' This from Roy Forette.

'Jerome. Know why? Your precious bank is busted, you crummy bastards, and every one of you is busted right along with it!'

They'd been waiting for this, half expecting it, but it shocked them into complete silence for almost a minute. Morgan glanced around at their faces. He saw disbelief in some, growing anger in others, outrage in a few. Carl Roushe was flushed and there was panic in his eyes. He spurred his horse, raced past Morgan and the sheriff and pounded away toward town. Forette and another man raced away to give

146

chase. Forette caught him before he had gone a quarter mile, leaned over and caught his horse's bridle, dragging him to a halt.

The column, which had spurred to a lope, caught up. Dan asked drily, 'Figurin' to get there first, Carl? Did you think you could get your money out before anybody knew something was wrong?'

'What if I did? Everything I've got in the world...' He stared at Dan, white-faced, defiant.

Dan turned his horse and faced the men. 'Get this straight. The bank is closed. It isn't going to open up today, or tomorrow, or any other day until the bank examiners have had a chance to come in and look things over. Get used to that. Because that's the way it's going to be.'

The men were grouped, now, before the sheriff. From somewhere in the bunch came the almost breathless words. 'You knew! For Christ's sake, you knew about it all the time!'

They stared at each other in bewilderment. Dan English made no denial of the accusation.

Roushe said, 'That can't be right. I've known Dan English for fifteen years. He's the sheriff. If he'd known, he'd have done something.'

Forette asked, 'What about it, Dan?'

Dan's shoulders sagged. He tried to meet the eyes of his accusers, but couldn't do it. So he looked down at his hands, clenched on the saddle horn. His voice was barely audible to those in back. 'Yes. I knew.'

Morgan saw Len Slaughter crowding to the front. Len's beefy face was almost purple with fury. 'You sold out. Damn you to hell, you sold us out!'

The sheriff shook his head. Morgan shifted his rifle slightly where it lay across his saddle. His right hand tightened on the receiver.

Dan English said, 'I didn't sell out!' His head came up briefly and he stared at the members of the posse. He conceded, 'Maybe I was wrong. I guess I was. By God, I should have arrested Jerome and the Gregos when I first found out what had happened.'

'Why the hell didn't you?'

Morgan moved. He gigged his horse and crowded up beside the sheriff. 'I'll tell you why. He was thinking of the town. He was trying to keep things going in the hope that Jerome could make good on what he took.'

'Ahhhh, don't give us that!' snarled Slaughter. 'He had his hands in the till just like everyone else. That saloon hussy, Lily, must come pretty high...'

Morgan's horse leaped under his gouging spurs. The horse's shoulder struck Slaughter's mount, which grunted sharply with surprise, and plunged away. Morgan put himself between the sheriff, who was trying to get at Slaughter, and Slaughter, who was too riled to care whether he mixed it with the sheriff or not.

Morgan shouted, 'Now calm down, the bunch of you!'

Slaughter bellowed in his face, 'Who the hell are you, to tell us that? A no good, goddam gunslick and a gutless one at that. Stay out of it, Orr. Stay out of Arapaho Wells, too, or we'll do you like we did that Grego bunch!'

Morgan's expression settled. So the guilt over this day's killings had gone even before the day was gone. Now it was a thing of pride, a thing with which to threaten others.

He let his glance shift from one to the other of the possemen. A dangerous quality of recklessness was building up behind their eyes, spurred on by the panic that had grown in them when they learned the bank was broke.

He glanced at Dan English. Dan's face was pale, but his jaw was hard-set, his eyes cold with determination and defiance. Dan knew this was probably the end of him, and he faced it without flinching. Curt Grego was watching, a mocking smile on his long, thin mouth. But his eyes held a sober fear, for he knew he was close to death as well.

Morgan shifted his eyes to Roy Forette. Roy was too young to have any financial interest in this, but there was excitement in him at the tension and potential explosiveness of the situation.

Balked, Slaughter bellowed, 'So what you goin' to do now, Sheriff?' He accented the word, 'sheriff' contemptuously. 'You goin' to let the Gregos and Jerome escape? Is that the plan?'

Dan English didn't dignify the accusation with an answer. He just glared at Slaughter. Obviously, Dan was rapidly losing control of himself.

Slaughter swung around. 'He don't even deny it. Because it's the truth. Looks to me like some of us had better take over. By God, I'm not goin' to take this lyin' down!'

There was a brief silence then, while Morgan watched their faces warily, seeing the quick decision each made within himself.

He whirled his horse, and when he reined in, he was side by side with Dan. He said under his breath, 'If you're going to stop them, Dan, now's the time to do it.'

Dan English didn't move or speak. A fair man, he knew there was justice in the anger of his possemen. He knew he had been wrong. His own feeling of guilt would hinder him from any effective action.

Morgan lifted the muzzle of his rifle. It centered on Slaughter's chest. He said, 'Whoa now, Len. Slow down. Grego's going to jail and Jerome's going with him. We'll catch Al.'

'Don't tell me what to do!' Slaughter shouted intemperately. Swinging around he yelled, 'Come on! Let's get 'em! Let's string Curt up and then go after Al and Jerome! Let's break into the bank and see how much of our money is left!'

Morgan said softly, as Slaughter paused for breath, 'Try it, Len, and my first bullet is going straight through your shirt pocket.'

He knew Len was going to move, but he hesitated a fraction of a second too long. Len spurred his horse, raising his rifle as he did.

The rifle blasted, not by design, Morgan was sure, but fired accidentally by a reflexive tightening of Slaughter's hand. He fired his own rifle over Slaughter's head. The man's horse began to pitch.

Morgan swung his head. Dan English had a startled look on his face. Greenish pallor was already staining his face.

He slid sideways from his saddle. Morgan caught him, steadied him while he slipped to the ground himself. He eased Dan down and laid him on the ground. Dan's face contorted now with agony.

Morgan unbuttoned his coat, knowing as he did there was no use. He could see the hole in the coat where the bullet had gone. Dan had bet everything he had on this hand, and he'd lost.

The posse was silent as death. Even their horses stood still, as though the shock of the men had communicated itself to them. Forette dismounted and walked to Morgan and the sheriff, his face blank with shock.

Dan grinned weakly. 'This is it, Morg. Tell Lily...'

Morgan said, 'I'll tell her. Better still, you tell

her yourself. You're not finished yet.'

He had forgotten the posse, forgotten everything but Dan English, dying so senselessly here on the cold ground.

Dan said, 'Don't wait too long, Morg. Don't be the fool I've been. Make up to Tena what you did to her six years ago. That little girl is yours, not Jerome's.'

Morgan heard a sound from Forette, standing behind him. Dan gripped his hand savagely as another spasm of agony twisted his face. Then his grip relaxed, and with it his expression. His breathing stopped.

Morgan knelt motionless on the ground for a moment. Then he rose and turned to face the posse.

The expression on Forette's face struck him like a stunning blow. Never in his life had he seen such concentrated hatred, such outraged, terrible fury.

For an instant it numbed him, blanked out his thoughts. And then suddenly, he understood. Roy Forette had heard the sheriff's dying words. Roy Forette was in love, with boy's idealism, with boy's worshipping, undemanding passion, with Tena Jerome. He thought Morgan Orr had wronged her, and now he had a holy, compelling reason for wanting to kill.

A sound like a growl came from Forette's throat. In an instant his hand would streak for his gun. And against the lightning speed

Morgan knew he possessed, a rifle pointed at the ground would be less effective than a stick.

Dimly, Morgan heard the pound of a horse's hoofs. He heard Len Slaughter yell, 'Grego! He's getting away!'

Forette's eyes flickered, distracted momentarily by Curt's escape, by that excited shout.

Morgan moved instantly, without thinking, like a striking snake. The rifle came up, and he lunged forward with it, viciously driving its muzzle into Forette's belly.

Forette grunted, and doubled, his face twisted with the knife-like pain. Morgan didn't wait to see him fall. Whirling, he seized the dragging reins of his horse. He vaulted to the saddle, set his spurs, and raced away.

Then he heard the sound—an animal sound that came from a dozen throats. It was the growl of a slumbering beast that is just beginning to awake. The sound was that of the just-born agony of a mob.

CHAPTER FOURTEEN

Morgan raced away. The horse Si Booth had given him was a good one, that now dug in, laid his belly close to the earth and ran. Behind him, Morgan heard the deep-throated, authoritative bark of a rifle.

He swung his head and looked around. Slaughter had raised his rifle and fired, with the muzzle of the rifle directly above his horse's head. The animal, terrified by the concussion, was pitching furiously again.

Slaughter dropped his rifle, and clung with both hands to the saddle horn. As Morgan watched, his grip broke and he plummeted through the air to land on his shoulders on the ground.

He dropped into a little swale, and the scene behind was hidden from his eyes. Morgan didn't delude himself that the trouble was over. But Slaughter's difficulties would hold back pursuit and give him a lead of half a mile. Which might be enough.

Ahead of him now he could see Curt Grego racing along. Curt was bent low over the withers of his horse.

The air was colder now. The wind whipped into Morgan's face with its frosty, wintry smell. He felt the sting of a single, tiny snowflake.

He glanced up at the clouds. Thicker now, they drove along close to the ground with terrifying speed. He hoped it would snow. He hoped they were in for one of those sudden, soaking, unseasonable blizzards that often struck the high plains country. A good soaking and chilling might cool off some of the hotheads in the bunch behind. He couldn't see the sun, but he guessed it must be close to two o'clock in the afternoon.

Morgan guessed he would make it into Arapaho Wells all right, barring a fall or something unforeseen, but getting safely to Arapaho Wells wasn't the whole answer.

He began to think of Mel Jerome, of Tena and the child. He doubted if Grego and himself could reach the town more than four or five minutes ahead of their pursuers. He'd have to forget Curt for now. He'd have to get Jerome safely to the jail before he did anything else.

He was counting heavily on the fact that the posse had not yet solidified behind a single leader. The possemen wouldn't be prepared for action when they rode into town. They'd want to gather others, and talk, and get a few drinks under their belts. They'd want a leader most of all, someone who could whip them up and weld them into a single, unthinking personality, whose thoughts were the thoughts of the leader himself.

Morgan frowned. Not a man of those behind him would admit it, but what they really wanted was to submerge their consciences in a conscienceless group, so that what they had to do, or thought they had to do, would be palatable to them.

Ahead, Grego pounded into a stream bed and startled a bunch of antelope that raced out of the stream bed and across the grassy plain.

Morgan's grain-fed stable horse was sweating heavily. Then, suddenly, the horse

155

put a foot into a prairie-dog hole, stumbled and went to his knees.

Morgan slipped his feet out of the stirrups as he felt the horse falter under him. He tried to leap clear, but was caught by the somersaulting horse and flung twenty feet ahead. The horse's flailing hind hoofs missed him by less than half a dozen feet.

He landed rolling, lost his rifle and hat, and stopped, sliding on his back. The wind knocked out of him by the fall, he lay there a moment, gasping helplessly. Pain ran through his chest, but at last he succeeded in drawing a breath.

Coughing, gagging, he got to hands and knees, peering around for the rifle. He saw it, got up and staggered toward it.

A shot banged out, and another, both going wild. Morgan looked up to see the hard-riding members of the posse coming on, now less than a quarter-mile away.

He snatched up his rifle, levered open the action. He put his mouth down over the breech and blew the dirt out of the muzzle. He didn't want the damn thing blowing up in his face when he fired it.

Snatching up his hat, he turned back toward his horse, which was now up.

He rammed a foot into the stirrup and swung up. He sank his spurs savagely and the horse leaped away.

Two more shots banged out behind, now less

than two hundred yards away. One of them stung the hindquarters of Morgan's horse and he began to pitch. Morgan got a firm grip on the saddle horn with one hand, holding up the animal's head with the other. He fought the startled horse into a run.

When he had succeeded, Morgan released his grip on the horn and took his rifle from beneath his arm.

Grego was now only a speck ahead. Behind, shots banged out sporadically, but none of the bullets even came close. Morgan's horse managed to maintain his lead, but he knew that wouldn't last. The horse had wrenched his leg in the fall and was beginning to limp.

Several more snowflakes struck Morgan's face. Staring ahead, he realized suddenly that Grego had disappeared. Still shaken from his fall, it was several moments before he discovered that the horizon had also disappeared—into a driving squall of snow. A few minutes later, he plunged into the swirling wall of the storm.

It was almost like plunging from one season into another. At first the flakes were small, stinging. But as he progressed into the storm, they became icy balls of driving sleet, and then great, wet flakes as big as a man's thumbnail.

His face and hands were soaked almost instantly. Sounds became muffled, unreal. The ground underfoot became wet and slippery and Morgan reluctantly drew in on the reins.

Limping, and uncertain because of it, the horse ran on. The pursuit began to fall behind. From two hundred yards, the distance between them lengthened to three hundred—four. Morgan drew in a little more on the horse's reins, until the animal was traveling at a slow, steady lope.

Now, the posse seemed content just to keep him in sight, and no more shots were fired.

The possemen didn't have to hurry, thought Morgan wryly. They knew the destination of their quarry. They knew their time would come.

*   *   *

Morgan's horse was floundering dangerously, when at last he saw the huddled buildings of Arapaho Wells dimly through the storm.

One good thing—the townspeople would be off the streets. It would take time to assemble them—maybe long enough for him to gather up Mel Jerome and get him safely to the jail.

He rode into the town and along Main without seeing a soul. Lamps burned in a few of the windows, and below the Second Street intersection, the dirty windows of both saloons were aglow.

In midafternoon, the town was dreary and gray, and yet again Morgan Orr felt the obscure menace hanging over it.

He wondered briefly if the storm would slow

158

things down when they began to happen. He doubted it. If anything it would make things worse. Wet and cold men are less inclined to be reasonable. Men drink more when they're wet and cold. By nightfall the men of this town wouldn't even be men any more. They'd be a howling, drunken mob.

Probably they'd break into the bank—loot it. And then the bank's chance to come back, to get on its feet again, would be gone forever.

Behind him, Morgan heard a flurry of shots, and several hoarse, hollow shouts. The storm tended to muffle both, but not enough. Morgan had heard them. Others in the town would also hear them. Sliding and skidding in the slushy mud underfoot, Morgan rounded the corner on Third and headed toward Jerome's house.

CHAPTER FIFTEEN

Curt Grego and his brother Al arrived at Jerome's house at almost the same instant, while Morgan was still a mile from town.

Snow still came down in great, wet flakes. The sky overhead was so dark it might have been dusk instead of midafternoon. Lamps winked from most of the windows.

The air was rich with the smell of burning cedar wood. Curt watched Al slide from his horse. He saw the brownish clotted blood in Al's hair and on his face. He crossed to his brother and said, 'Bullet creased your skull, huh?'

Al nodded ponderously, grimacing with pain as he did.

'Head ache?'

'It aches like hell.'

'What'd you come here for?'

Al grinned, proud that his own idea had been the same as Curt's. 'Same thing you came for. Money. How'd you get away?'

'Never mind. Come on. We haven't got much time.'

He opened the gate and went up the walk. He knocked imperatively on the door, waited an instant and knocked again.

A voice called out from behind the door, 'Who is it?' and this was the voice of Jerome's wife, strong and steady, but filled with fear.

'It's Curt Grego. Open the damn door before I blow the lock off.'

There was a short hesitation. Curt heard a man's deep tones and the door swung open. He stepped inside and Al crowded in behind. Fear touched Tena's face as she saw him, as she saw the blood on Al.

Jerome stood beside her, half afraid, half angry. Curt said shortly, 'Get your coat. We're going down to the bank.'

'What for?'

'Damn you, don't argue with me. The whole

160

thing's out. The sheriff's dead and the mob's right behind me. They're going to string you up.'

Jerome's face lost every vestige of color. Panic filled his eyes. He started to whirl.

Curt smashed his fist into Jerome's mouth. 'Damn you, come on!' Jerome staggered back, but this time he didn't try to run. He stood there staring stupidly at the pair.

Curt looked at Tena. 'You come too. Maybe they'll go a little easy with their guns if they know we got a woman with us.'

Tena said unflinchingly, 'I'll get my coat. I want to go.'

She got her coat, and brought Jerome's. She helped him into it. He seemed dazed, unable to think.

Curt opened the door and shoved them outside. He and Al followed. As they passed the horses at the gate, Curt said, 'Leave 'em! They're played out anyhow and maybe it'll slow things down if that damned posse thinks we're holed up inside.'

They tramped along the snowy street, seeing no one. Turning the corner onto Main, Curt heard a horseman coming. He shoved Jerome and Tena into a doorway. He seized Tena and put a dirty hand over her mouth. She struggled helplessly, making small, muffled sounds.

Jerome didn't move to interfere. Al grabbed him and muffled his mouth with a hand, holding a forearm locked tight around his throat.

Morgan thundered into sight and wheeled around the corner to head for Jerome's house. Curt released Tena. 'Get going.' He pushed her out onto the walk. She slipped, and nearly fell.

Jerome walked swiftly toward the bank, making no move to help her. Al and Curt came behind.

Reaching the bank, Jerome unlocked the door. Curt took the key from him and locked it behind them.

The bank was dark and musty smelling—faintly redolent of stale cigar smoke. Curt said harshly, 'Guns first. Where are they?'

'You'll take me with you? You can't leave me behind. They'll hang me!'

'Guns. Where are they?' Curt looked at Jerome with contempt.

'There's a revolver in the cage—a shotgun in my office.'

Curt said, 'Watch 'im, Al.' He strode swiftly through the gate, circled behind the cage and came out an instant later with the revolver. He said, 'Go open the safe.'

Jerome's expression was hidden by near darkness, but his voice held scared defiance. 'Nothing doing. Not unless you promise to take me with you.'

Tena broke in, 'Mel, you can't open the safe for them. You can't just give up the town's money like that.'

Curt laughed shortly, 'He's dead if he don't. And you are too.'

Jerome's voice trembled, still defiant. 'I won't do it. Not unless you take me with you!'

'Maybe this'll change your mind.' Curt swung a flat-handed blow at Tena. It struck the side of her face and knocked her sprawling. Jerome didn't move.

Curt stepped over to him and smashed him full in the mouth as hard as he could. Jerome slammed against the partition, tearing it loose, and crashed to the floor. Curt walked over and kicked him deliberately, savagely, in the belly. 'Open it up,' he said implacably.

Jerome got to his hands and knees, gagging. He nodded dumbly. Curt said, 'Help him up, Al.'

Tena screamed, 'Mel, they'll kill you! As soon as you open that safe, they'll kill you!'

He didn't reply. With Al's help, he shuffled toward the rear of the bank. Curt dragged Tena to her feet. Pushing her ahead of him, he followed the pair. At the door of Jerome's office, he stopped, went inside, and returned a moment later with a shotgun cradled under one arm.

Jerome squatted in front of the safe. Even in semi-darkness the violent trembling of his hands was visible. Curt said savagely, 'Hurry up, you son of a bitch!'

Jerome began to twirl the dial. Tena stood shivering, waiting. She knew they were going to kill Mel. She knew, too, that when they did, they'd kill her too, or worse, take her with them as a hostage.

Soundlessly, she began to pray.

* * *

Morgan's horse was blowing hard as he ran along the quiet street. He swung down at Jerome's house, fear striking him instantly as he saw the two horses tied before it. He recognized Curt's mount. He guessed the other was Al's. Al was tremendously strong and big. A creased skull hadn't apparently stopped him or even slowed him down.

Morgan ran up the walk, rifle in hand, fully aware that at any instant gunfire from the windows might cut him down. But he was also aware of the shortness of time. The posse was right at his heels. If they came to Jerome's first...

Crossing the porch, he moved as silently as a cat on padded feet. He tried the door, and was surprised to find it unlocked. He slammed against it, plunged into the house and hit the floor rolling.

Nothing happened. No sound marred the utter stillness. He stood up. 'Tena,' he called softly, and louder, 'Tena!'

No answer. No sound.

For a moment he stood motionless in the darkened house. Had Jerome fled town, taking

Tena with him?

It was possible, even probable. But that didn't explain the two horses tied out front. It didn't explain the absence of Curt and Al.

All three men knew the game was up, he reasoned. All three knew they had to leave or die. It was much more likely that Curt and Al had come here, picked up Jerome and Tena, and left.

But they'd need horses. Probably they'd need money too. It wasn't likely that Jerome kept very much in his house.

Morgan plunged out the front door. He ran out to the street. Looking down, he saw four sets of footprints in the snow—heading toward Main. One was smaller than the others.

The sky seemed darker than before. He was soaked and chilled, but he scarcely noticed it. His mind was going ahead, as his eyes followed the tracks on the walk. In some places they were already drifting in with snow.

Muffled by the storm, but still plainly audible, came the low, angry murmur of the combined voices of many men. Looking ahead, Morgan saw them dimly, coming up Third toward Jerome's house.

They marched along in the middle of the street, an angry clot of men, looming suddenly out of the storm before Morgan had time to duck out of sight.

He tried to brazen it out, by turning unconcernedly in at the nearest gate, like a man

165

returning to his home. But one of the men in the vanguard of the mob yelled, 'Hey! You! Come 'ere and let's see who you are!'

Morgan broke into a run, ducking between two houses. A shot racketed in the street. He halted in the shelter of an enormous lilac bush and held his breath.

Snow from the heavily laden bush sifted down on his head and back. Out in the street a man shouted, 'Slaughter, you an' Roushe take a look. See who that was. The rest of us will go on to Jerome's.'

Morgan waited soundlessly, hesitating between staying and hoping they'd miss him in the storm, or making a run for it.

The two men came toward him so fast that he had no choice but to stay. He held his breath as they passed within a few feet of him and then started silently in the direction from which they had come.

Hurrying along, Morgan's mouth twisted wryly. He wasn't exactly making friends in Arapaho Wells. So far, he'd managed to antagonize most of the townspeople, one way or another. Not an auspicious start toward building himself a new life. He grinned ruefully. New life, hell! He'd be lucky if he hung onto the one he had.

He was remembering the way they'd all opened up almost hysterically at the Grego place. He was perfectly aware that the same thing could happen right here in town. They wanted Jerome, the Gregos, Morgan himself. And most of them wouldn't care how they got them, nor even if a few innocent bystanders caught stray bullets in the process.

Ahead, suddenly, he saw more dark shapes materializing out of the driving snow. Reinforcements for the mob, he guessed. Men who had held back at first, but who had now worked themselves up to the necessary pitch.

Morgan whirled, vaulted a fence, and sprinted for the passageway between two houses. He could cut through to Main...

A shout lifted, 'There! There's one of 'em! Get the son of a bitch!'

Morgan knelt beside the house and flung the rifle up. He aimed over their heads and pulled the trigger. The gun clicked. He fumbled for fresh shells, found his pocket empty. He'd lost them somehow, probably back there where the horse had spilled him.

He got up, flung the rifle away. Weaponless, he lunged away toward the alley. Turning the corner, he heard a rifle bark behind him. The bullet plowed a long furrow in the snow.

He blundered into a pile of crates stacked between the houses and fell headlong. Rolling, scrambling, clawing in the icy, slushy snow, he made it to his feet, flung himself through a gate and into the alley.

Behind him, the rifle roared again, this time tearing a chunk out of the rotting backyard fence. Another gun flared, its sound flatter and less deafening than the first. A revolver. Morgan didn't hear that bullet strike at all.

He lunged out onto Main and saw that he had come out into the street a few doors up from the hotel. The bank was close, but between Morgan and the bank was a knot of half a dozen more men, arguing, effectively blocking his way. They glanced upstreet in time to see the four pursuing Morgan come trooping out of the passageway.

One of the other four yelled, 'It's Jerome! Cut him off!'

Morgan was neatly boxed between the two groups. He glanced frantically up and down the street, searching for another passageway which might put him into the alley behind the hotel and give him a chance to elude his pursuers. There was none.

Guns in both groups flared, and in front of Morgan, glass store windows shattered and tinkled to the ground. A man shouted, 'Hey! Cut it out! You just shot out the window of my store!'

Morgan felt an almost hysterical desire to laugh at the ridiculousness of it. Concern for a store window when they were shooting at a man—when they didn't even know they were shooting at the wrong man!

Taking a wild chance, Morgan jumped— straight through the shattered store window.

He found himself in a small dry goods store. Counters ran along both sides and down the

168

middle. He tore along the dark aisle and as he ran, he tipped over the center counter so that it fell crossways in the aisle. Bolts of cloth and notions tumbled with it. He grinned to himself. In a minute he'd hear the man who had been so outraged over the breaking of his window literally screaming as the muddy boots of ten men trampled through his store and over the top of the spilled goods.

He slammed into the tiny back room, which was also piled high with goods. If the storekeeper had a padlock on the back door ... well, he'd be boxed in here and wouldn't have a chance.

He heard them coming in the front before he reached the door. He heard the storekeeper's outraged voice ...

He reached the door. It was securely padlocked.

Frantically, he glanced around. There were some high windows that opened from the top.

He leaped up on a pile of boxes and fumbled for the catch. A gun roared up in front, sounding inordinately loud in the enclosed space.

The window stuck, then opened so suddenly that Morgan lost his balance. The stack of boxes began to topple.

He seized the window frame and yanked himself up. The boxes crashed, falling away from under him.

His weight, on the hinges of the top-opening

windows, broke them at last and gave him a clear shot at the opening. He fell on through, landing on back and shoulders in the alley.

He was up immediately, and as he plunged away, he heard someone fumbling with the padlock inside the door. And a great deal of balked and angry shouting.

He ran swiftly along the alley, limping a little on one ankle that he'd twisted in the fall. His back burned like fire from the bits of brick dust and lead buried just beneath his skin. But he had to reach the bank. If he never did anything else, he had to reach the bank!

CHAPTER SIXTEEN

He would never have made it but for the fact that he had drawn almost every man in the street into the wrecked dry goods store. Now those inside milled around in the back room and the few who remained in the street out front rapidly crowded inside, believing that they had Jerome trapped.

Morgan swung left into Second, glancing briefly at the sheriff's office and jail across the street. It was hard to believe that Dan English was dead. But it wasn't hard to believe that this was a town wholly without law in his absence.

Ahead he could see the bank dimly through the gathering darkness and the driving storm.

He ran toward it steadily, trying to quiet the ragged run of breath in and out of his starving lungs.

He reached the intersection. He could hear the racket issuing from the dry goods store and knew that any moment men would come streaming from its door. He saw no one, so he crossed the street, walking now, taking great, long breaths into his lungs.

He stepped into the bank doorway and tried the door. It was locked. Stepping back, he kicked it solidly beside the lock. It shook, but did not give.

There was glass in the center of the door. Morgan kicked again, and this time glass shattered and tinkled to the ground.

Expecting shots momentarily, Morgan kept working on the glass until he had an opening large enough to get through.

He put a leg in, careful of jagged shards of glass clinging to the doorframe. As he did, a shotgun blasted somewhere in the depths of the bank.

Birdshot peppered Morgan's leg, but his head and chest were behind the protection of the shattered door and jamb.

He dived through recklessly, feeling the run of excitement in him. His guess had been right. Curt Grego was here in the bank, and Al, and probably Jerome and Tena too.

As he hit the floor, rolling, the shotgun roared again. This blast shattered the front window. A big plate glass window, it came tumbling down, both inside the building and out, with a thunderous crash.

Morgan kept rolling, trying to see in the darkness. His eyes caught a flicker of hooded light from the rear of the bank. It was nothing more than a faint glimmer on the high, ornate ceiling, but it was enough.

He came to hands and knees, and lunged toward the rear of the bank. As he crashed noisily through the gate, a revolver flared. The bullet missed but struck the gate as it swung to behind him.

Morgan, flat on the floor, marked the location of the flash in his mind. It had scarcely faded from his eyes before he was up, moving again, but this time noiselessly, with all the stealth of a stalking cat.

His eyes were now more accustomed to the lack of light, and he saw the towering iron safe against the wall. He saw several figures before it. He couldn't tell whether it was open or not.

He heard Curt Grego's harsh whisper, 'Kill that damned light,' and almost instantly what little glow there was from the hooded lamp disappeared.

Curt's voice again, 'Out the back, Al. Hurry up. Bring those two along.'

Morgan abandoned caution and ran toward the back door. He reached it ahead of them and stood against it, waiting. He had no gun and without one had no chance. But he wasn't going to stand by and see them go without even giving them some opposition. Besides, though he couldn't yet be sure, he figured they had Jerome and Tena with them.

Bluff might work where force could not. His voice was steady as he called, 'Come on, Curt. Come on. This is the end of the track for you.'

The revolver flared. The bullet tore into the wall three feet from the back door. Morgan made no sounds. Maybe he could get Curt rattled enough to make him go out the front door. If he did that, one of the townsmen, drawn from the dry goods store by the shooting and breaking glass, was sure to get him.

Curt shouted hoarsely, 'Take that woman, Al, and head for the front.'

That almost made Morgan move. If they took Tena for a hostage ... The men in the street wouldn't care. They'd shoot first and think afterward.

Then he heard Jerome's voice, 'No! Don't! For God's sake ...!'

There was a brief scuffle between Morgan and the front door. The revolver blasted again, and a heavy body thumped on the floor. Movement didn't stop. There were clawing, thrashing sounds, and a man's steady, continuous groaning.

Curt had shot Jerome. Tena screamed, and Morgan heard Al's low-voiced cursing.

He lunged forward recklessly. He passed the

173

lumped, groaning shape of Jerome on the floor, and then, against the gray in the shattered front windows, saw the silhouette of a man.

He dived at Curt's legs, felt himself strike, heard Curt's startled exclamation. Curt went down heavily. The gun clattered against the floor.

Morgan grabbed for him blindly in the darkness. He felt his hands touch Curt's leg, then felt it yanked away. Curt was up, running toward the door.

Morgan, frantic now, bawled, 'Al, turn her loose or I'll blast you!' Al wasn't quick witted. He was used to taking orders. He might release Tena without thinking.

In the darkness, he couldn't tell what was happening. And there was no time to hunt for the gun Curt had dropped. Morgan ran toward the door, scared worse than he had ever been in his life. If Al dragged Tena into the street ... in this light, the townsmen probably wouldn't even realize he had her. Even if they cared.

He reached the door, which now gaped open. He heard a little cry to one side of him. Then Tena was against him, weeping from shock and hysteria.

The snow had stopped outside. The clouds had thinned slightly, and there was a little more light in the street than had been there before.

Morgan saw Al and Curt crash into a running townsman, knock him down. Al scrambled to his feet. Curt struggled briefly with the man on the ground. When he stood up, he held a gun in his hand. With the other he still clutched the canvas bag containing the bank's money.

He yelled, 'All right! Get going! I've got a gun!'

Off to the right, over in front of the hotel, a rifle cracked. Curt apparently didn't notice. Al lumbered into motion, with Curt immediately behind him.

And then Morgan heard a voice he recognized. It was Roy Forette, who stepped out from the livery stable door. 'Hold it! Drop the gun!'

Curt shied aside like a horse that has spied a snake. His arm swung and the revolver in his hand shot flame from its muzzle.

But Morgan was watching Forette, who did not even have a gun in his hand.

Forette stood solidly, legs slightly spread. He was tilted forward ever so slightly. His right hand blurred, and almost instantly his revolver was in his hand. Flame licked twice from the muzzle.

Al, who had been immediately behind Curt, went down, face first, in the slushy street. Curt didn't even look at him. He swung hard to the left and disappeared into a passageway between two store buildings. Forette lunged after him.

Men streamed past the door of the bank. A

couple stopped and knelt over Al's body lying in the street. The rest, yelling wildly back and forth, disappeared in pursuit of Curt and Forette, like a pack of dogs hot on a scent.

For an instant, Morgan stood there motionless. He doubted if he had ever seen a man draw and fire faster than Forette had done. Not only that, even in this poor light, Forette had scored a hit.

This was the speed of youth. Morgan might match it if he was in top physical condition. The way he was today, he wouldn't have a chance.

He became aware of Tena. She controlled her weeping long enough to sob hysterically, 'Mel! They shot him!'

Morgan released her and she ran toward the place where Jerome still lay. Morgan followed.

Jerome was conscious. Tena knelt on one side of him, Morgan on the other. Morgan fumbled for a match, found one and struck it, using his body to shield the light from the street.

Jerome's upper left arm was a mass of blood and torn flesh. Morgan said shortly, 'Arm wound. He'll be all right. Wait until I find that gun and we'll take him to jail. We can tie it up there.'

Holding the match cupped, he got up and searched for the gun. He found it, checked the cylinder and discovered it was empty. He said, 'Where does Jerome keep shells for this?'

'In the cage, I think. Probably one of the drawers...'

He hurried into the cage. He yanked out three drawers before he found the shells. He loaded the gun quickly, stuffed the box of shells in his pocket.

Returning he hoisted Jerome to his feet. The man cried out sharply with pain. Morgan pulled the man's uninjured arm over his shoulders and started for the door. Tena walked on the other side, steadying Jerome's hurt arm.

Going out the door, Morgan suddenly thought of Tena's little girl. He said, 'Where's Serena. Was she ...?'

'She went with Sophronia for the afternoon. I'm supposed to pick her up at six. She's all right.'

The commonplace. The cook takes a little girl for the afternoon. In that space of time lives are wrecked, men killed. And it wasn't even six yet.

Morgan slogged along the middle of the street, heading for the jail. He held Jerome's left wrist in his left hand, the man's arm around his neck. He held the gun in his right. The jail was his only hope—the only place in Arapaho Wells where Jerome might be safe.

The distance between Main Street and the jail seemed like twenty miles. The pace of the past twenty-four hours was telling on Morgan heavily now. First there had been that beating

177

in the Buckhorn Saloon. Then the ride out to Grego's place. Then the ride to escape the posse and the fall ...

He was panting heavily. Tena couldn't help much without disturbing Jerome's arm.

Behind him, in the distance, Morgan could hear the shouts of the men pursuing Curt Grego. They seemed to be coming closer.

They reached the jail at last. Morgan tried the door and found it unlocked. He steadied Jerome against the outside wall. Tena took over to hold him up while Morgan went inside.

He lighted a lamp first. Then he went out and helped Jerome in. He sat him down in the sheriff's swivel chair. He returned to the door and locked it, dropping the heavy bar into place.

Tena, her face ghastly, was tearing Jerome's sleeve away from the wound. Morgan took out his knife and cut it away with a half a dozen swift, sure strokes.

He looked at Tena's face. It was gray, but her mouth and eyes were steady. He said, 'Sit down. I'll get bandages and a bottle of whisky.'

The bandages were in a cupboard against the wall. Whisky he found in the sheriff's bottom drawer. He uncorked the bottle and handed it to Jerome, who took it dazedly, drank, choked and almost dropped the bottle. Morgan took it from him. He wadded up a handful of bandage, soaked it with whisky. He poured raw whisky over Jerome's wound.

Jerome yelled, but Morgan held onto his arm. He began to sponge the wound with the whisky-soaked handful of bandages. Jerome jerked on his arm, screamed and fainted.

Morgan wound bandages around and around the arm. They were instantly soaked with blood, but it was a slow, steady flow, coming from veins and not from arteries.

When he had finished, he picked Jerome up and carried him back to one of the cells, where he laid him on a bunk. Tena followed and covered her husband with blankets.

Morgan drew her from the cell and locked the door. He followed her back to the front office.

He sat down, soaked, muddy, beat and out of breath. He glanced at Tena, who had collapsed into another chair. She was trembling violently. Her lower lip quivered, and her eyes brimmed with tears. Wanting to hold her, to comfort her, was a need that almost seemed like physical pain.

There was a smear of mud on one of her cheeks. Her gown was sodden with mud for a foot above the ground. Both her hands were muddy from falling.

He said, 'When you feel up to it, go get the doctor.'

She looked at him beseechingly. He knew she wanted to stay. He said, 'I wouldn't let you stay here anyway.'

Tena's head lifted. Her eyes sparkled. 'I'm

going to stay here! I've got to!'

Pervading the air of the room suddenly was a sound—like the buzzing of thousands of flies—like the whirring wings of hundreds of birds. Morgan strode to the window and stared through. He saw, in the light of the lanterns, that the street was almost solid with the dark shapes of men. Suddenly a rock struck the window before him.

He ducked back to avoid the flying glass. Out in the street Len Slaughter's voice bawled, 'Send him out, Orr. By God, you send him out!'

Morgan opened the door. Silence fell in the street. Morgan said, 'Go on home. Jerome's hurt and locked in a cell. I'd think the bunch of you would have had enough bloodletting for one day. Have you forgotten the sheriff? And Chuck's woman? And Chuck?'

He saw his father break out of the press of the crowd. Sam had a bottle in his hand which he held by the neck. Sam yelled drunkenly, 'What the hell is everybody waitin' for? He's only one man! Come on!'

He started toward Morgan, weaving drunkenly. He slipped, staggered, and then abruptly sat down in the mud, a ludicrous expression on his whiskered face. Somebody laughed, and the laughter spread. Sam tipped up the bottle to take a drink and fell on his back in the mud and snow. The laugh grew in volume.

Morgan said, 'All right, one of you go get

Doc. The rest of you go on home. Jerome will be here when it's time for the trial. You can count on that.'

'What about Curt? He's got all the money that was left in the bank!'

Morgan wanted to taunt them with their failure to catch Curt. He knew how it had been. Curt was dangerous as a wolf with his foot in a trap and they'd given up because they figured Jerome would be easier. But he didn't taunt them. Instead he said, 'We'll get up a posse in the morning. We'll get Curt then. Now go on home.'

He backed into the office and closed the door. He turned to face Tena Jerome. Her lips were moving soundlessly. Morgan said, 'It's all right. It's all right now.'

But his eyes were worried. He knew it wasn't going to be that easy. The trouble wasn't over yet. Before tonight was over, he had to face Roy Forette, and that was a fight he knew he couldn't win.

CHAPTER SEVENTEEN

Tena was shivering as though she were cold. Morgan crossed the room and began to build a fire in Dan English's pot-bellied, cast-iron stove. It caught immediately and began to roar softly. He left the door open to more quickly warm the room.

Tena came across to the stove and spread her hands to catch its warmth. She stared moodily into the flames. 'I can't help feeling that this is my fault. If I'd been the wife I should...'

Morgan didn't answer. He wanted to reassure her, to tell her that nothing she could have done would have changed anything. But he knew this reassurance was something she would have to find within herself.

Morgan stepped to the window and peered outside. He pulled back at once, his face gray and without hope. The men in the street were not dispersing, not talking, not even moving around. They were just standing there looking at the jail.

He fished absently for his tobacco, and found it wet. He crossed the room, got a sack from the drawer of the desk.

He made a cigarette and lighted it. He looked at Tena. He realized that both of them were waiting. Tense, scarcely breathing, they were waiting for the sound to grow and swell outside.

And the mob was waiting too, waiting for some one man to take control. Morgan had thought Len Slaughter might be that man, but now he knew differently. No. It was Dillon they were waiting for, Dillon, who was driving the wagon with the bodies of the Grego family in it.

The room was warm now, so Morgan closed

the stove door and the damper in the pipe. He said, 'Dillon ought to be driving in pretty soon.'

He crossed the room and sat down behind the sheriff's desk.

Tena paced back and forth, nervous and shaken. Morgan ached to get up and take her in his arms, but he didn't move. After a moment she turned and looked at him. Her face was pale, her lips bloodless. 'You don't have to stay. I haven't any right to ask you to stay—to risk your life ....'

He said, 'I'll stay. And everything will be all right. Wait and see.' He tried to sound sure, but he wasn't.

He had never been unsure of himself, and being so now was disturbing. Yet he knew one man's chances of holding the jail were slim.

In addition, Morgan realized that he had no real authority in the eyes of the people of the town. He would *have* to use his gun to inspire their fear and respect. And if he did that there was a good chance they'd get completely out of hand, destroying not only Jerome and Morgan, but possibly Tena as well.

Suddenly a roar went up out in the street. Morgan crossed quickly to the window, pulled aside the blind, and looked outside.

It was a few moments before his eyes became accustomed to the almost complete darkness beyond the lanterns outside. Then he saw Dillon's hulking figure striding down the street. He heard Dillon's shout, 'What's goin' on?'

The men outside clustered around him. Morgan saw that Sam Orr had gotten up out of the mud and was now standing, still with the bottle in his hand, weaving and peering owlishly at the jail.

Dillon stepped out from the others and faced the jail. He shouted, 'Morgan!'

Morgan went to the door, taking time first to seize a double-barreled shotgun and load it. He opened the door and stepped outside. Tena picked up the rifle and stood beside the open door, listening, trembling.

Dillon yelled, 'Give the son of a bitch up, Orr! We mean business. Just walk on out of there and you won't get hurt.'

Morgan yelled, 'I'm not walking out of here and you're not getting your hands on Jerome. Now go on home and sleep it off.'

Dillon roared, 'Sleep what off? You reckon when we wake up the bank will be all right?'

Harsh laughter echoed his sally. Morgan bellowed angrily, 'You think it'll be any better if you try to get in here and take Jerome?'

'Mebbe not, but we'll feel better!'

That was greeted with a muttered roar of approval. The mob surged forward, pushing Dillon ahead of it. Morgan raised the shotgun. His voice was deep and normal, but panic was growing in him. If only Tena were safe somewhere ... 'Hold it! Don't think I won't

184

fire, because I will. I'll shoot right into the bunch of you!'

The threat stopped them. For almost a minute the mob and Morgan faced each other, motionless, silent. Then someone shouted from the back of the crowd, 'He won't shoot! Go on, take him!' Heads in the front swung around. A man shouted, 'Open up and let 'em through. Let him go first.'

The crowd opened, but no one came through. Morgan shouted, 'Go on home now, boys. This whole business will look different to you tomorrow. Jerome's going to get what's coming to him. So's Curt when we catch him!'

'What about the bank? You goin' to fix that too?'

Morgan didn't reply. Muttering started in the rear of the mob. Morgan turned disgustedly and slammed the door. He growled, 'No damn use standin' there arguing with them.'

Back in the cell block, Jerome began to yell. Morgan went to the door and opened it. Tena followed him.

Jerome was standing against the bars, clutching one with his unhurt hand, which was white-knuckled with strain. His face was bathed with sweat, and his eyes wild with fear.

'Get me out of here! They'll tear me to pieces!'

Morgan said unsympathetically, 'Shut up! They're not goin' to get you.'

'You're lying! You're only going to hold out long enough to make it look good. Then you're going to let them in!'

Tena went to the bars and stood looking up at Jerome. 'Mel, it's all right. Morgan's doing all he can.'

'Sure! He'd like to see me dead! So would you! I know what the pair of you are up to!'

Tena flushed painfully. She looked up steadily into his eyes however, without flinching. 'Mel, I swear to you, I'll never let you down. If you get away, I'll go with you. If you go to prison, I'll wait!'

Jerome laughed mockingly, bitterly, but there was a note of hysteria in the laugh too. He released the bar, put a hand through and pushed Tena viciously. 'Who the hell wants you?'

Tena staggered across the corridor and slammed against the bars of the opposite cell. Jerome looked at her. Tears suddenly filled his eyes and his mouth began to work like that of a small boy about to cry. He whirled and ran to the cot. He sat down heavily and began to sob brokenly.

Morgan took Tena's arm and led her out to the front office. She was white, trembling, but there were no tears in her eyes.

He closed the door separating the office from the cells and sank wearily into the swivel chair. Tena faced him. 'Was he right, Morgan. Are you going to give him up?'

Morgan scowled at his boots, hesitated a moment and then looked up. He tried to examine his own motives, his own desires. He wanted Tena, needed her, and the need showed plainly in his eyes. She flushed at the intensity of his glance, but her eyes didn't waver.

Did he want Jerome dead?

Morgan met Tena's eyes steadily. He said truthfully, 'I want him dead. I want your husband dead and I want what's mine—you—my daughter. I won't play games with you or with myself. But I'll not hand Jerome over to that mob. I won't have a hand in his death. He'll stand trial in a regular court or I'll die with him. Does that answer you?'

'Yes, Morgan.'

'I wonder where that damned doctor is.'

'Maybe he's out of town on a call.'

Morgan shrugged. 'Maybe. Not much he can do for Jerome that I haven't already done anyway.'

Tena sat down dejectedly in a straight-backed chair. Morgan went to the window, pulled the blind aside slightly, and stared outside. The crowd seemed smaller than it had a few moments before. He wondered if some of them had become too cold and discouraged and gone on home. It didn't seem likely.

He could see no hope, no future for himself. Even if he survived the night, even if he succeeded in turning back the mob, the events of the night would make it impossible for him to stay here in Arapaho Wells. Hatred for him would be too strong.

Nor was there any hope for him where Tena was concerned. Troubled by guilt over her deception of Jerome six years before, she'd now be undeviatingly loyal to him even if he went to prison for life.

He should never have returned, he realized now. Jerome's mistaken fear that he had been sent to check into Rossiter's disappearance had precipitated the present crisis. Sooner or later it would have happened anyway, but by then the bank might have been in better shape.

Struck by an idea he had, Morgan stepped to the cell block door, opened it and went inside, closing it behind him. He stood at the bars and said, 'Jerome!'

'What do *you* want?'

'How short are you at the bank?'

Jerome sat up. There was a certain defiance in him now, a compulsion to appear well to Morgan. He said sarcastically, 'I suppose you've got the cash to make it up!'

'No. You know better than that. I just wondered if you'd managed to make any of the losses good.'

Jerome shook his head.

'How much are you short?'

'Thirty thousand, counting what Curt Grego took.'

'Any chance those mining claims will ever be worth anything?'

Jerome shrugged. 'I thought so when I bought them.'

Morgan turned away. He returned to the office and closed the door behind him. He had hoped Jerome had at least bettered his position, by however small a margin, in the past six months. It would have been a talking point with the mob.

He went to the window and pulled aside the blind. It was completely dark outside, and still snowing. Lanterns still winked in the street, illuminating the scene.

A dozen men stumbled along the street, carrying a log about thirty feet long.

Morgan swung his head. 'They've got a battering ram.'

Tena came up beside him at the window. She stared out bleakly.

Morgan looked at the door. It was built of two-inch oak planks, probably taken from some wagon bed when the jail was built. Heavy strap iron hinges reached all the way across the door, bolted to each plank. He decided it would hold a while, provided the repeated blows of the ram did not loosen the door casing and tear it free.

Tena looked up with terrified, imploring eyes. 'What are we going to do, Morgan? Oh God, what are we going to do?'

'The best we can. If that door holds, they'll probably get tired after a while and go on home. It's pretty cold and wet out there.'

'How about the window? Can't they...'

Morgan shook his head. 'It's too small, for one thing. And it's got bars across it. Even if they could get the bars out, only one man could come through it at a time. So they won't try that.'

He wanted to touch her, to hold her close. He clenched his fists involuntarily with his effort to control the desire. He said, needing desperately to know this, 'How has it been, Tena? Has he been good to you?'

'That's not fair, Morgan. Not now.'

'No. I suppose it isn't.' He looked at the bleeding cut on her temple, made when Jerome had pushed her.

He found he didn't hate Jerome. Rather he felt toward the man a mild contempt. Jerome had been cowardly and spineless throughout the affair—first by stealing from those who trusted him—then by having Rossiter killed. His breakdown in the cell had given Morgan a slight feeling of nausea. Yet he knew the cowardice and weakness in Jerome was his greatest strength where Tena was concerned. It would insure her loyalty.

Outside, now, a roar went up, and immediately thereafter, the battering ram struck heavily against the door. A cloud of dust, accumulated over the years in the hard, cracked wood, sifted away from the door. Morgan, standing beside it, stepped away and sneezed.

The ram struck again. And again. Over against the wall, Tena began to sob softly, and back in the cell block, Jerome began to hammer with something on the bars.

Morgan picked up the shotgun, broke it and checked the loads. He walked to the window, broke the shotgun again and checked the loads a second time.

His hands were shaking slightly. He wondered if he'd be able to shoot into the men outside. He knew that as soon as he pulled aside the blind, he'd be irrevocably committed to the course he had sworn to take.

And he couldn't help thinking of the townspeople, couldn't help wondering which of them would be struck by the shotgun blast.

In a torture of indecision, he looked first at Tena, then at the cell block door. In his eyes was his effort to weigh the life of Jerome against the lives of the men outside. But it wasn't a case of weighing the one against the other, and he knew that too. It wasn't a case of which was most valuable but a principle of whether law or mob rule would prevail in the end.

Jerome began to shout hysterically and Tena got up impulsively. Morgan crossed the room and stood in front of the cell block door. He said implacably, 'No. You can't do him any good. Stay out of there.'

She faced him determinedly for a moment. Then wearily she turned and returned to her chair.

Outside, Dillon's great voice bellowed, 'Open up, Orr! Open up, by God, while you still can. That door won't hold forever. I'll give you five minutes. If you aren't out then, we're comin' in!'

CHAPTER EIGHTEEN

For a long time after that, utter silence held. Morgan no longer hesitated over what he would do. He knew. He would be defending not only his own life, but that of Tena and the prisoner. He would be defending the only regularly constituted law in Arapaho Wells. He would shoot to bluff at first, but if that didn't work, he would shoot to kill. This would be a day long remembered in Arapaho Wells. Hatreds that could never die would be born of it. And he knew this too—most of the hatred would be directed at him.

He breathed harshly, waiting out the allotted five minutes. Tena trembled violently as though from cold, but she made no sound. Back in the cell block, Jerome blubbered intermittently like a child, and between times cursed savagely.

Outside the sound began to grow again. Morgan glanced at the clock on the wall. Two minutes had passed.

He heard Dillon's harsh shout in the street. 'Hold it now! I gave 'em five minutes and it ain't up yet!'

Five minutes. Five minutes to break their nerve. Morgan thought briefly of how easy quitting could be. All he had to do was to throw open the door and walk outside. It was half a block to the hotel. All he needed to do was to take Tena to the hotel and wait. It would be over in less than half an hour.

Except that he knew it would never be the same. His self respect would be gone—his pride with it. Tomorrow, when the full shame of what they had done hit the townsmen, they'd hate Morgan for letting them do it. And Tena...

He crossed the room, dumped a box of shotgun shells onto his desk and stuffed a handful of them into his pocket. He looked at Tena, his mouth a thin, straight line. 'Think I ought to give him a gun?'

'I don't know. If you think...'

Morgan stared at the floor. He looked up grimly. 'If they pick up that battering ram again, I'll put a load of buckshot into them.'

'Then Mel doesn't need a gun.'

Morgan glanced at the clock again. The five minutes were almost up.

Morgan felt very much alone. He turned to the window and pushed aside the blind. As he did, a yell went up outside. Dillon shouted, 'Time's up, Orr. You comin' out, or are we comin' in?'

Morgan ripped the shade off with an impatient gesture. He shoved his body hard against the bars and poked the snout of the double-barreled ten gauge out the window. He didn't shout, but his voice was plainly audible in the sudden hush out in the street. 'Neither. Touch that ram again and I'll shoot.'

Dillon bawled, 'All right. You heard him. He ain't goin' to give 'em up. So we got to take 'em!'

The men hesitated briefly, looking from Dillon to Morgan and back again.

He saw his father standing out there, swaying a little but more sober apparently than he had been before. Dillon roared, 'Come on! Come on!' and slogged through the slush to where the log lay.

Sam Orr scuttled after him, his mouth working, his eyes catching the glow of the lanterns on the boardwalk. They seemed strangely bright, and lusting as he seized the butt end of the log and tried to lift.

He barely stirred the log, but a lead had been all the others needed. They scrambled for the battering ram, lifted it, and surged toward the door. Sam held on drunkenly, steadying himself on the log.

Morgan lifted the shotgun. 'Drop it! Damn you, drop it or I'll shoot!'

His only answer was a howl of derision from the street.

He raised the shotgun to hip level, pointed it loosely at those holding the ram. The range was about fifteen feet, point blank for a ten gauge loaded with buck.

The shotgun roared, its muzzle yanked up slightly just before it fired. Those holding the ram stopped as though they had run into a wall. Before they could drop the log, Dillon's voice roared, 'He fired over your heads, and that's all he'll ever do! He won't shoot into you, no matter what he says. Now hit the door and let's get this over with!'

The men steadied and came on with the ram. It struck the jail door with a jar that splintered one of the oak planks.

Morgan released a long, slow sigh, like that of a dying man and raised the gun again.

It bellowed thunderously. Morgan saw Slaughter driven against the log, saw him double as he struck it, saw him tumble to the ground on the other side. Len's chest was a red horror from the full weight of the buckshot charge that had struck it.

Screams mingled with shouts of alarm and shock. In front of Len, two others went to their knees and then collapsed to the slushy ground. Beyond him, a man clapped a hand to his thigh and went hopping away, only to slip and fall, groaning.

Morgan broke the gun. The empty shells clattered to the floor. Acrid smoke curled up from the shotgun breech.

He fumbled in his pocket for fresh shells. He dropped three or four before his trembling hands could insert two into the gun. He closed it with a snap.

Tena began to sob hysterically, but she didn't move from her chair. A silence came over the street, broken only by the groans and cries of the wounded.

Morgan cleared his throat and said harshly, 'Pick up your dead and wounded and get the hell out of here. Don't come back.'

Someone at the rear of the mob flung up a revolver and emptied it at Morgan. Bullets slammed into the door, the window frame. One of them took a shard of glass that still clung to the frame.

Sam Orr, staggering between Morgan and the shooter, fell soddenly, face down in the mud and slush. He didn't move. Morgan felt an odd certainty that Sam was dead. He hadn't slipped; he hadn't passed out. He'd caught one of those wildly triggered pistol bullets.

A man ran to Sam and rolled him over. He looked up. 'Sam's dead too.'

Morgan stood at the window, frozen, shocked. Not by death; he'd seen that before. He guessed he was shocked by seeing his father die. But there was no real grief in him—there can be no grief where there is neither love nor respect.

He returned and found Tena staring at him piteously. 'Who?' Her voice was a whisper.

'Len Slaughter. And Sam.'

'Killed?'

He nodded. She kept watching him, compassion and terror mingling in her face. He said, 'A couple more are down. Buckshot wounds, but nothing bad. Maybe they'll give up now.'

He sat down wearily behind Dan's desk and leaned the shotgun against it. The revolver in his belt gouged him. He took it out and laid it on the desk. He fumbled the sack of tobacco he'd taken from Dan's desk from his pocket and rolled a smoke.

Tena asked almost soundlessly. 'Then it's over, you think?'

Morgan shrugged. 'I don't know. It could be. At least it's over for a while. They'll lug their wounded off to the hotel. They'll lay Sam and Len Slaughter out someplace. Then they'll either go home or back to the saloon to get tanked up some more.'

He was thinking that Sam Orr, who, during his whole life had earned nothing from this town but contempt, would now, along with Slaughter, become it's martyr—at least for tonight—at least while feeling ran high and the intoxicant of violence ran in the townsmen's veins.

He was thinking uneasily of something else—of Roy Forette. Even if he drove off the mob there was still Roy to be reckoned with. And Roy would not be driven off.

Back in the cell block, Jerome was yelling hysterically. Morgan went to the door, opened it and said savagely, 'Shut up. Go lie down and pass out. They're not coming in.'

Jerome stared at him unbelievingly. He ran his good hand through his tousled hair. There were tears on his cheeks and his mouth trembled like a woman's. Morgan shut the door, feeling somehow unclean for having looked at Jerome.

He crossed to the window and peered outside, aware of the chance that someone would take a potshot at him.

The battering ram lay where it had fallen. It was drenched with Len Slaughter's blood, as was the muddy ground where he had fallen.

Lanterns moved up the street, illuminating the retreating mob, illuminating the way for those who carried the wounded and the dead. They were already half a block away. They had left one lantern behind. It sat on the boardwalk near the abandoned battering ram and smoked and flickered dismally in the rising wind.

Morgan stepped to the door. It had been cracked and bent, and it took all his strength to raise the stout oak bar. He unlocked the door, stepped into the street, picked up the lantern and blew it out. He set it down against the wall, wondering where Forette was, how soon he would come. Almost angrily he turned, went back inside, closed and barred the door behind him. Now it was time to wait.

It was just a little after six o'clock. Tena said, 'I'm sorry about your father.'

Morgan glanced at her with surprise. He said shortly, 'Thanks.' He stared somberly at her for a moment, wishing he could make her leave, knowing he could not. At last he said, 'They're coming back, and I won't be able to shoot into them again. I wish you'd leave.'

She shook her head stubbornly. Her eyes said that if she couldn't live with him, she'd die with him. He felt a sudden tightness in his throat.

'Are you going to give Mel a gun?'

He nodded. 'If I can't protect him, I guess he's entitled to something to defend himself with. I'll let the mob know he's got one too. Maybe they won't be so anxious when they know there's a gun behind that door.'

He made another smoke and inhaled it slowly. This morning he had sat in the sun on the hotel veranda, listening to the church organ and the singing voices of the congregation. Now five men and a woman were dead by violence and the violence had not yet spent itself. Morgan had little hope that either he or Jerome would get out of this alive. His mouth twisted with wry self-mockery. He'd sworn he was going to stay in Arapaho Wells. It looked like he was going to do just that—with a headstone to mark his permanent place in the town. Forette had better hurry, or he'd lose his chance at Morgan. The mob would

199

get him first.

The clock ticked maddeningly on the wall, its brass pendulum moving back and forth relentlessly. Tena kept looking at it, and at last she said, 'How long do you think they'll wait?'

'An hour. I don't know. They were pretty wet and cold. They hadn't eaten supper, and some of them probably didn't get dinner.'

There was silence between them, then, for a long time. Morgan was thinking of what might have been—if he'd known six years ago what he knew tonight. Tomorrow, Tena would be alone, without a dollar to her name. How would she care for herself and for Serena? She couldn't stay here. The town wouldn't let her. But how could she go away, without even stage-fare to the next town?

Morgan began to feel a vague kind of anger rising in him, like smoldering, half-dead coals with a wind blowing them to life.

Like the muttering of thunder on a distant horizon, he heard the sound of the mob coming again.

His body was cold; his mind seemed numb. He said, 'I'd better get back there and give Jerome a gun.'

CHAPTER NINETEEN

He crossed to the racked rifles. There were some drawers beneath the rack. Inside one of them, he found a revolver and belt. He loaded the revolver and strapped on the belt. Then he picked up the small revolver he had found on the floor of the bank, crossed to the cell block door and opened it.

Jerome looked up dully from his cot. He was still sweating heavily, but he seemed in better control of himself than he'd been before.

Morgan poked the gun through the bar, butt first. Jerome didn't move. Morgan said, 'They're coming back. I don't suppose this is the right thing to do, but if I can't protect you, I guess you're entitled to some way of protecting yourself.'

Jerome wouldn't get up. He seemed incapable of moving. His eyes rested dully on Morgan, making the same accusation he'd made earlier.

Anger stirred in Morgan. He stooped and laid the gun on the floor inside the bars. Then he turned and tramped back through the door.

He closed it behind him and crossed to the window. As he stuck his head out, he saw the first of them round the corner from Main. There were more lanterns among them now. Most of them had changed to dry clothes, and a few weaved unsteadily, as though intoxicated.

They carried either shotguns or rifles, and there was a grimly determined air about the way they walked that boded no good for either Jerome or Morgan Orr.

There would be no more standing in the window and blasting into them with a shotgun, even had Morgan been willing to do so a second time. This time they would kill him as he appeared in the barred window with his gun.

He stepped over to the desk and blew out the lamp. He heard Tena's sharp intake of breath as the lamp went out. Her voice, however, was steady and determined. 'Give me a gun, Morgan.'

'No.' He felt her beside him. He turned. Suddenly she was in his arms, warm, soft, alive. She was weeping softly, and her cheeks were wet with tears.

He'd had so little of her, he thought bitterly. A night six years ago. And this. But it was his own fault he'd had no more. He realized that too.

He kissed her and his arms tightened convulsively. He couldn't help the unwilling thought that crossed his mind. The mob was going to get Jerome anyway. Angrily, he pushed the thought away. All his life he'd been doing the wrong things. This once, he was going to do what was right.

Tena whispered, 'I wouldn't have thought

this could happen. I know every one of those men out there in the street. I know their families and their troubles. I grew up with some of their children. But I guess I don't really know them at all.'

Morgan pushed away. 'You knew them when they were normal and they're not normal anymore. Some men change when they're drunk. Some change out on a hunting trip or a posse. Maybe it's a kind of primitive thing that's in them all but doesn't often show.'

Tena laughed shakily. 'Philosopher!'

There was a quality of waiting in Morgan now that puzzled him, a tension he did not understand. His scalp crawled and his chest felt hollow.

He had never been a man of temper, and could not remember ever having been uncontrollably angry. But the core of smoldering anger in the back of his mind seemed to be growing, as a fire grows, awaiting only the provocative breath of wind to make it leap to consuming heights.

The buzz of the mob's voice grew louder, and louder, and light from their lanterns gleamed in the broken window, laying dim patterns of its bar-crossed shape on the walls and floor.

Dillon's great voice bawled, 'Orr! Come out the door with your hands up. Bring a gun with you and we'll cut you to pieces!'

Morgan didn't move. Beside him, Tena

trembled violently. But she made no sound.

Dillon bawled again. 'Come out! Come out the door! If you come to the window, we'll cut you down!'

Still Morgan didn't move. Outside, Dillon ordered, 'Some of you get ahold of that ram. The rest of you cover the window. If anybody shows in it, shoot 'em down!'

There was a moment of confusion outside, then the ram struck the door a shattering, resounding blow. Morgan clenched his fists. It was time now to make up his mind, once and for all. Either he was going to stay in here and shoot every man who came through the door, or he was going to give up.

And then, a sudden, new sound startled him. It was a shot, deafeningly loud, back behind the door that led to the cell block.

Morgan crossed the room at a run, burst inside and closed the door behind, so that light would not seep out into the front part of the jail, also so that Tena couldn't see.

Jerome lay on the floor of his cell, the whole side of his head blown away. The revolver lay several inches from his hand, smoke still curling up from its muzzle.

Morgan had hated this man, had wanted him dead. He had felt little more than contempt for Jerome's cowardice. But he had not wanted it to end this way. Technically, Jerome had shot himself. But suddenly to Morgan the only reality was that the mob had succeeded. They had executed Jerome as surely as though they had put a rope around his neck. Without trial—without conviction, without law, they had executed their man.

And now they beat upon the door of the jail, still wanting blood, still wanting to kill and destroy. They had destroyed the personification of the law in killing Dan English. Now they meant to destroy the law itself, which they'd do if they forced the jail.

Fury burst suddenly in Morgan's brain. He slammed through the door, colliding with Tena who was trying to enter it. His voice was strange, and seemed to come from someone other than himself. He said, 'He's dead. Your husband's dead. And by God, this has gone far enough!'

If it was killing they wanted, he'd show them killing. If he had to die, he'd make his death costly. No longer did he think of the mob as men, as individuals, but as a faceless entity in itself, a conscienceless thing that would destroy and kill until its ghoulish appetite had been sated.

Oddly enough, it didn't even occur to him to try placating the mob by announcing Jerome's death. Holding them off had become a principle with him, a principle he could not now betray.

He stooped and tied the thong at the bottom of his holster to his thigh.

The gun was like a piece of precision

machinery. He slipped it in and out of the holster several times. Not as fast as his own, but fast. Fast enough for anybody but Forette.

He removed the revolver and checked the loads in it absently by the dim lantern light flickering through the window. The battering ram struck again. The doorframe moved with this blow, and mortar dust sifted to the floor.

Morgan crossed to it. Anger still boiled in his mind, but a steadiness had come to him, the old, familiar steadiness that always came to him when he was moving into a fight.

He waited beside the door, no longer conscious of Tena's presence in the room. The ram struck again, and again; the door planks splintered. Once the ram came through and stuck, and it was several minutes before the men outside could yank it loose. There would be an instant, Morgan knew, after the door went down when the men outside would be off balance, off guard. There would be a split second while they geared themselves to rush inside and meet the hidden gun of Morgan Orr. In that split second, Morgan intended to leap outside.

There was a strong possibility that reflex would direct the charges of half a dozen shotguns into his body. But there was also a chance that surprise would freeze them long enough. Upon this he would bet his life, as he had bet it upon his judgment and skill so many times before.

Endlessly, now, the ram crashed against the door. It gave by fractions of inches with each hard blow. Dust filled the room, dust from disturbed mortar, dust of a score of years' accumulation.

Morgan resisted the need to cough and waited, seemingly indolent beside the door. And outside in the street, the roar of the mob mounted as excitement and anticipation gripped its members.

Morgan thought briefly of Roy Forette, sure that Forette was out there, aware that upon Forette's actions depended the success of his plan, his very life or death.

The door sagged. The top hinge parted, leaving an opening at the top six inches wide. Morgan's body tensed.

He heard Dillon's roar, 'Another one now. Another one and down she goes!'

The ram struck again, but the stout old door did not go down. The gap widened at the top. Morgan could see out through the gaping crack now, could see the lanterns, the bright, lusting eyes and twisted faces of the members of the mob.

A craziness was on them, the same craziness they had displayed last night when they attacked him in the Buckhorn. Sleeping savagery had come awake, burning through the thin layer of civilization and decency.

Seeing them thus helped the resolution in Morgan Orr, strengthened him in his determination to stop them, to save the last remnants of law and order that remained. He could face them, and kill if necessary, with no regret. For he would not be killing decent law-abiding men. He would be killing savages.

They were striking the door, now, at its lower extremity, trying to burst the second hinge. The stout oak bar across the door, the bar Morgan had thought would hold, was wrecked, and the bolt which secured it at one end was pulled almost through the solid masonry wall.

Another couple of blows ...

But it took only one. The ram struck the bottom of the door and the hinge popped like a pistol shot. The door tottered for an instant and then fell inside the room with a resounding crash.

Instantly Morgan leaped through the opening and stopped on the walk before the door, legs spread, knees bent almost imperceptibly.

His right hand hung, limp except for a slightly bent elbow, beside the sheriff's holstered gun.

The howl, which had begun as the door crashed, ceased suddenly, and the street was, for an instant, as still as death. Morgan's voice, though not raised in a shout, carried well in the silent street. He said, with deadly matter-of-factness, 'The first man that raises a gun or takes a step dies.'

Bunched before him, they froze. They stared at his implacable eyes, at his tight-drawn mouth, at the gun he wore.

They knew—they saw one thing in the face of Morgan Orr. He would do precisely what he'd said he would. He would kill the first man that raised a gun or took a step toward him.

And though they could not know it, he was not fighting for the life of an embezzler, a murderer. He was fighting to keep a semblance of law alive in the town of Arapaho Wells. He was fighting disorder and anarchy. Because if the town humbled and destroyed its law this once, it would do so again—and again.

But this they could see—a quality of inner forcefulness about the man who stood before them that was beyond the threat of his gun, a quality possessed by few but one which engendered fear and respect too vague to be connected with thoughts of specific physical violence.

Seconds dragged, and even the harsh breathing of the men who had wielded the ram became shallow and almost still.

The smallest simultaneous movement on the part of several of the men could have broken the deadlock. Morgan could not have stopped them all. But in each man that faced him was a sudden, very personal fear of death. Each man knew that if he moved he would instantly die.

Into the deadlock, into the breech, suddenly stepped Forette, the one man who had no fear, who hated Morgan for what he thought Morgan had done to Tena Jerome. With his gun holstered, he stepped to the forefront of the crowd and stood there with smoldering eyes. 'Take me first, Morg.'

Something cold lay against Morgan's spine. He had lost, and would die. He had seen Forette's speed. Rested and strong, he might have matched or beaten it. Now he knew he could not.

Half a minute passed, half a minute of breath-held, silent tension.

And then, the awful silence was broken by a voice, a woman's quiet voice that held determination and a deadly threat. 'Roy, if you touch that gun, I'll kill you.'

There was the slightest of sounds at the shattered window. Morgan didn't swing his head, but he could feel her presence there. Until now, she had been helpless to help him. Now she was no longer helpless.

Confusion stirred in Roy Forette's eyes. He swung his glance to Tena in the window, seeming for this instant to forget Morgan altogether. 'You mean you'd kill me for *him*? After what he's done to you?'

Morgan swung his head and looked at Tena's face. She turned and met his eyes. All her love for him, all her longing, was suddenly very plain in her face. Morgan knew that if he died tonight he would have had this at least. Tena looked back to Forette and said quietly,

'Yes, Roy, I would.'

Roy stared at Tena, studying her face in the flickering lantern light. The battle he fought inside himself was plainly visible. But when he swung his eyes again to Morgan, there had been a subtle change in his expression. He stepped toward Morgan and, reaching him, turned to face the crowd. He said, 'Go on home. If Morgan gets the first, I get the second. Now does anybody still want to try?'

Morgan felt the sudden warmth of gratitude. Gone was the feeling that he would have to kill, that he would certainly fail in the end. He could taste the exhilaration of success.

They knew Roy was fast, and he was one of them. They knew the almost legendary speed of Morgan Orr. They accepted and swallowed the bitter certainty that between the pair half a dozen men would die when the mob began to move.

Morgan said steadily, 'Those in back peel off and head for home. One at a time, as Forette calls your names.'

Not a sound broke the silence of the street. Forette began to call off names, and one by one the men at the rear of the mob broke off and plodded up the slushy street. Forette waited between names long enough so that there was more than a hundred feet between each departing man.

Minutes ticked away. The size of the mob dwindled steadily as its cowed members slunk away.

Dillon was last. And yet, even in Dillon, the leader of the mob, there was no defiance left. Savagery, the lust to kill, seemed gone from the man entirely. Once again he was the town blacksmith, a man with children and a wife, a man who yesterday had sweated over his forge and who would again, tomorrow.

He splashed away through the mud and slush. Morgan watched until he turned the corner onto Main.

Inside the jail, Tena had relighted the lamp. Morgan stepped through the ruined door, with Roy Forette following soberly at his heels.

Tena ran sobbing into Morgan's arms, and he held her, long and hard. Then he turned to Roy. 'Dan deputized us both, and I guess it holds. You stay here and watch the jail. I'm going after Curt.'

'Tonight?'

Morgan nodded. 'The clouds are thinning. The moon will come up soon. With mud underneath two inches of slush, a trail ought to be easy enough to follow.'

Morgan turned to Tena. 'Go on up to the hotel. I'll see you as soon as I get back.'

She opened her mouth to protest, all her fear for him standing out plainly in her eyes. But she did not protest. She must have seen how important this was to him. Perhaps she understood that finishing this properly was his way of making himself a place in the

212

community.

She went out, looked back at the door and smiled tremulously. Morgan turned to the sheriff's desk. Opening one of the drawers, he took out a tarnished deputy's badge.

He pinned it on, conscious of Forette's eyes upon him. He stepped out into the snowy street, walked to the livery barn, got a horse from Si Booth and rode out.

He had no idea where Curt had gotten a horse, but was sure he had. One thing was certain; Curt hadn't stayed in town.

The rising moon made an eerie glow on the thinning clouds overhead. Morgan circled the town, and at last picked up the plain, hard-traveling prints of a running horse leaving it.

The exhaustion of the day was catching up with him. Every muscle in his body ached. His mind seemed dull and slow to think, and he knew this was the result of the terrific tension he had been under during the past few hours.

What would Curt Grego do? Would he run as fast and as far as he could? Or, like a wily, malevolent wolf, would he lay a trap for those who pursued him?

Morgan tried to gauge the hatred that was in Curt Grego. Curt had seen his two brothers and his brother's wife killed. Morgan remembered the look that had been in Curt's eyes as he viewed the carnage out at their shack in the cedar hills.

Morgan slowed his horse instinctively. He

was still less than three miles from town. Curt had, he decided, passed the point where his own life and safety mattered. Curt would have laid an ambush somewhere along the trail he had made. Curt was waiting out there now, hoping to take as many of the men from town as possible with him when he died.

Being sure of this, Morgan was suddenly glad he'd gotten Jerome to jail and held the mob there. Because if they'd taken this trail, a lot more of them would have died.

Now, Morgan himself had to be bait for Grego's trap. He knew of no way he could spring it other than to ride on Curt's trail and wait, ready to leap from his saddle at the first sound of shot, hoping that in this poor light, Curt's first shot would miss.

He had thought the showdown with the mob in town had taken all his strength. Now he found a reserve of strength somewhere. A few more hours—and then it would be all over. Arapaho Wells was a ruined town, however this came out. But maybe there'd be a place in a ruined town for Morgan Orr. Maybe he could be around still when the town came back.

The clouds kept thinning, and the moon laid a cold, bright glow upon the land. Morgan made a plain, black target as he rode across the dazzling expanse of snow.

Ahead, there was a ridge, strewn with cedars, with a narrow shelf of rimrock at its top. The trail climbed up the side of the ridge.

Morgan touched his horse with his spurs. The animal jumped ahead, lunged up the side of the ridge.

And then, fire shot from the muzzle of a rifle a hundred yards ahead.

Morgan's eyes caught the flare, and his body leaped into motion instinctively, before the actual significance of the flare had registered on his mind. He heard the bullet hit the saddle, heard the horse's shrill snort of fright. He was out of it, then, rolling in the snow, his gun in his hand.

And suddenly, for the first time in his life, anger took over his actions completely. An unthinking machine of destruction, he leaped to his feet and charged, afoot, straight up the slope toward Curt Grego and his waiting rifle. The strain of two days' iron control had been too much. Now, when caution might have saved his life, he flung it to the winds and charged.

Slipping, sliding, floundering on the slippery ground, he lunged ahead. The rifle flared and he snapped a shot at it, heard the bullet strike a rock and ricochet off into empty space.

Seventy-five yards—fifty. His lungs were afire, but his mouth was hard, his eyes like bits of stone. Moonlight seemed to magnify his size, to increase his apparent speed.

Curt lost his head. He stood up behind the rock that had sheltered him, flung the rifle to his shoulder, levered and shot as fast as he could. He screamed, 'Damn you! God damn you! Die! You're a man, ain't you?'

One of Curt's bullets tore through the fleshy part of Morgan's thigh. Another ticked his sleeve, raking a long shallow gash along his forearm.

Twenty-five yards. Revolver range now. And Curt, calmed at last, stood rock still and aimed the rifle unswervingly at Morgan's chest.

Morgan skidded to a halt. As he did, his gun came up, centered and bucked against his hand. Curt Grego's rifle blasted deafeningly.

But Morgan felt no bullet shock. Instead, he saw Grego's knees buckle, saw Grego collapse, jackknife forward and strike the rock before him with his face and chest.

He walked on up to where Grego lay. He knelt and put a hand on Grego's chest.

Then, wearily, he rose and stumbled past Grego up the hill until he came to Grego's horse, tied in a clump of cedars. The bank's canvas bag hung from the saddle horn.

Morgan took the sack, leaving the horse tied. He staggered down hill to his own horse, mounted and set a course for town.

Blood soaked his pants and ran down into his boots. But it was over! It was over at last. Suddenly all the trouble of the past two days made sense and seemed worthwhile. He headed straight for town, riding as fast as the pain in his thigh would let him, a man with a

216

goal, now, and a place to go and stay.

CHAPTER TWENTY

The snow melted and briefly muddied the streets, and then dried under the persistent, beaming rays of an autumn sun. At sundown, two weeks after the attack on the jail, Morgan Orr limped slowly up Second and paused at its intersection with Main to shape and light a cigarette.

The outgoing stage pulled up before the hotel in a cloud of dust. Lily Leslie stepped down from the hotel veranda, a bag in her hand.

Morgan grinned and crossed the street. He smiled approvingly at Lily and helped her into the coach. She said, 'Good-by, Morgan.'

'Good luck.'

She smiled, a trifle ruefully. 'Maybe I'll need it. But the label's coming off, Morgan. You made it, and now I can too.'

Another man stepped down from the hotel veranda, a dry little man with gold-rimmed spectacles pinched to his nose. His hand was small and limp in Morgan's big one. He said briskly, 'The bank will open tomorrow on a limited withdrawal basis. In time, I suspect, those mining claims that Jerome speculated in will pay off in full. Good-by, Mr Orr.'

Morgan watched him climb into the coach. He glanced across at the bank, then back down Second toward the jail. His long mouth made a thoughtful smile.

Roy Forette was down at the jail, wearing a polished deputy's badge pinned to his vest. Morgan was not the only one in Arapaho Wells who had found a place.

The stage pulled out in a billowing cloud of dust. The sun sank in the west, briefly staining the clouds a brilliant orange.

Morgan stepped down into the street and crossed, occasionally nodding pleasantly to one or another of the people he passed.

He turned on Third, with but a passing glance for the big two-storied house where Tena and Jerome had lived and went on, all the way to the end of the street.

Here, at the gate of a small, white frame house, he turned in, his eyes lighting with anticipation.

A little girl, her nose glued to the window, watched him gravely as he came up the walk. As he stepped onto the porch, she gave him a shy, slow smile, then disappeared like a wild thing from the window.

Morgan twisted the bell and waited. He heard Tena's light footsteps hurrying to the door.

It opened, and Morgan stepped inside. For a moment they stood looking into each other's eyes. Then she was in his arms, and her mouth

218

was soft and warm beneath his own.
Morgan Orr was home at last.

We hope you have enjoyed this Large Print book. Other Chivers Press or G. K. Hall Large Print books are available at your library or directly from the publishers. For more information about current and forthcoming titles, please call or write, without obligation, to:

Chivers Press Limited
Windsor Bridge Road
Bath BA2 3AX
England
Tel. (01225) 335336

OR

G. K. Hall
P.O. Box 159
Thorndike, Maine 04986
USA
Tel. (800) 223–6121 (U.S.
In Maine call collect: (207)

All our Large Print titles a
easy reading, and all our b
last.